Orphans of the Wind

Orphans *of the* Wind

ERIK CHRISTIAN HAUGAARD

Illustrated by Milton Johnson

HOUGHTON MIFFLIN COMPANY BOSTON

Books by
Erik Christian Haugaard
HAKON OF ROGEN'S SAGA
A SLAVE'S TALE
ORPHANS OF THE WIND

CONTENTS

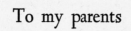

To my parents

The Captain of the *Four Winds*

1

"ENGLISH SHIPS are sturdy, well built . . . No better masts nor stronger sails are made anywhere, but the sailors!" The man who was speaking sniffed and stared at me, as old Judge Wicks stares at the criminals before he sends them to the gallows.

I looked down at my bare feet. From one of my trouser legs a thread hung; its end lay curled on my big toe like a white worm.

"Cutthroats! Permanent lodgers in jail! That is what the English sailors have become!"

"Now . . . Now, Captain Mathews, you were unlucky on your last voyage. The English sailor may be rough, but he is the backbone of our nation," said Mr. Pond and glanced nervously out of the dirty window of his office. Mr. Pond was the chief clerk of Morgan and Son, Shipping and Sea Supplies. He was a gaunt man, with a solemn face which — though I knew him well — I had seldom seen creased by a smile.

"Then, Mr. Pond, unlucky I was! For a more lazy crew than my last, you could not find in Seville, nor a more thieving one in Vera Cruz."

"Foreigners." Mr. Pond pronounced the word in such a way that it became a curse.

"No, Mr. Pond, good Englishmen all of them; and

it will surprise me if many of them escape meeting their Maker at the end of a piece of good English hemp."

"Captain Mathews, in Jim, here, you will get a good deck boy. His mother was a hard working woman; she did washing for my wife."

Uncle Robert — so I had called Mr. Pond when my mother was still alive, for his wife and my mother were sisters — beckoned for me to step forward. I walked half the distance between myself and the two men. The captain was sitting in a chair beside the desk, next to which my uncle was standing.

"Step forward, boy." The captain's face was fat and still red from anger. As I walked up to him, I kept my gaze on the bottom button of his coat. "Who was his father?"

Captain Mathews turned his head towards my uncle, and I looked up at him for a moment, deciding irrevocably, as children do, that I did not like him.

"His father was a sailor. He was drowned when the lad was only six months old. He never saw him."

The captain grumbled as if he had heard of a crime I had committed. "How old is he?"

My uncle spoke very hastily. "Thirteen," he said.

For a moment I thought of confessing that I was only twelve; but the thought of the beating I knew my uncle would give me, should I prove him a liar, kept my mouth shut.

"I think he would make a better chimneysweep than a deck boy," the captain said. Then he grabbed my arm, to judge if my rags covered any muscles at all.

"As a favor . . ." The captain nodded. "As a favor to you, Mr. Pond, I shall take him." Rising from his chair, he shook hands with my uncle. Then he looked once more at me. After remarking offhandedly, "He can come aboard tonight," he left the office.

"The sea," my uncle said, as soon as the door closed behind the captain, "is a great opportunity. Captain Mathews is a great sailor. His boat, the *Four Winds*, is only a brig, but it is a good ship. You should thank me for what I have done for you."

My mother had died two months before, and since then I had been busy thanking either Mr. or Mrs. Pond for the food I ate, the rags that I wore, and the beatings I received.

"Ingratitude . . ." My uncle looked up at the ceiling, which once had been white but now was blackened with soot from the lamp. "Ungratefulness is one of the vices. Ungratefulness is the signpost that leads to jail."

I did not say anything; for in fact, my uncle never expected me to. I was trying with the toes of my one foot to tear the thread that was hanging loose from the trousers of the other.

"Jim, are you listening?"

I nodded my head and mumbled, "Ungratefulness leads one to . . . to . . ."

"Jail!" my uncle repeated severely; but then — perhaps because he really believed that I could end

my days in such a place — he walked over to me and placed both hands on my shoulders. "Remember your mother, my lad."

My dislike of my uncle always turned to hatred when he mentioned my mother. Since her death not one night had I gone to bed dry-eyed. "Yes, sir," I whispered as I felt the tears forming.

"I shall have to buy you some clothes. You have proved a considerable expense to me, lad."

"Yes," I murmured. Now the tears were gone.

"William," my uncle called, standing at the door of his office.

A tall youth, with reddish hair, came to the door. He stood there for a few seconds, then he bent his head slightly in a bow.

"Take this boy down to 'Hawkins' on Old Field Road, and have him outfitted. But tell old man Hawkins that it is work clothes the lad wants; and the bill must not come above two pounds."

My uncle turned and looked down at some papers on his desk. I did not know whether I ought to say "thank you"; so I stood motionless until I heard the red-haired youth call me.

"Come along, boy."

I started towards the door. I was under the archway when my uncle coughed. I looked back, my uncle had raised his gaze from the papers and was watching me.

"Thank you," I muttered. My words made my uncle frown.

"It is a great opportunity."

I nodded, for I knew not if my uncle meant that going to sea was a great opportunity or getting new clothes at Hawkins'. "I shall make arrangements with Captain Mathews to subtract the two pounds from your hire."

I nodded again, but I must not have appeared pleased, for my uncle added, "Debt is a millstone around a man's neck. It drags him into the sea of usury."

"Yes, sir," I replied.

"After tea tonight, I shall take you down to the ship, myself."

As we walked out of my uncle's office the red-haired young man instructed me to walk *behind*, not *beside* him.

Old Field Road was near the harbor, not far from my uncle's residence at the bottom of Grandby Hill. Mr. Hawkins' shop was on the street floor of an old house. It smelled of tar and other sea gear. "Old man Hawkins" I did not see, but "young" Mr. Hawkins appeared older than my uncle.

When the red-haired youth, who had ordered me to call him Mr. Clark, informed Mr. Hawkins of my uncle's request, he threw up his hands in despair. "Mr. Pond wants a sailor outfitted for two pounds: for forty shillings!"

Mr. Clark shrugged his shoulders.

"Why not try Mr. Lesley's establishment on Bran-

don Hill? Why so modest as to come here with your order? Under three pounds, I cannot do it."

I was ready to leave; but Mr. Clark took a small stick from one of his pockets and stuck it between his teeth, while he mumbled, "The lad is just to have work clothes."

"Fancy that, just work clothes . . . And what if the Queen invites him to dinner?"

Mr. Clark removed the stick from his mouth, looked long at Mr. Hawkins, and drawled, "The boy is an orphan, shipping out with the *Four Winds*. The *Four Winds* ain't Buckingham Palace." Mr. Clark pronounced Buckingham Palace as a Londoner, though he was born and bred in Bristol.

"An orphan . . ." Mr. Hawkins peered at me, as if I were a native of a tribe he had never heard of. "The *Four Winds*, eh?"

I bobbed my head up and down; and Mr. Hawkins smiled kindly at me. "You will learn to work, my lad."

Mr. Clark threw his stick on the floor and said, "Hard work never hurt anybody."

Mr. Hawkins looked at him, as if he had first seen him now. "Then, my lad, you should have a go at it, too. I shall outfit you free, if you will sail on the *Four Winds*."

Mr. Clark sat down on a roll of rope that stood near the door. "Will you outfit him, or won't you?"

"Come here, my lad." Mr. Hawkins waved his arm and I followed him to the back of the shop. There, on great shelves, seamen's clothes were arranged

according to sizes. Even the smallest of the canvas trousers were much too big for me.

"Maybe they will shrink," Mr. Hawkins said without too much conviction, as he rolled up the legs.

I was well outfitted for two pounds, though I only got one — or when necessary, a pair — of each thing. Mr. Clark said, "Since everything was twice as big as it ought to be, it was as good as getting twice as much."

With a duffel bag over my shoulder, I departed from Mr. Hawkins' shop. Mr. Clark did not bid me good-bye, but winked his right eye, as he walked away. I started towards Grandby Hill, but had only gone a few steps when I heard someone shouting behind me. I turned around and saw "young" Mr. Hawkins running after me. As soon as he realized that I was standing still, he stopped running and I noticed that his legs were very short.

"My boy, a knife! You can't go to sea without a knife." In his open hand, the "young" Mr. Hawkins held out to me a beautiful knife. Its broad and sturdy blade was encased in a leather sheath and the handle was inlaid with mother-of-pearl.

"But I can't pay for it," I said; yet I kept looking at it, for I had never owned anything so valuable.

"You may have it." The middle-aged man pressed the knife into my hand, turned around, and walked rapidly away.

"Thank you!" I called after him. "Thank you!"

I took the knife to my lips; and forgetting where I was, I kissed it; then I hid it inside my trousers, for fear my uncle might discover that I had it.

The Cook of the *Four Winds*

2

MY UNCLE OWNED a small house at the foot of Grandby Hill. It was an ugly house — or, at least, I thought it was an ugly house — for it smelled of the sour food of poverty. Not that my uncle was poor, but he was a miser and would not part with a penny without hoping to get twopence in return. Now, food that you eat and clothes that you wear, are merely expenses. That, in any case, is the way my uncle looked upon them; therefore, one ate as poorly in his house as the vagabonds did at the workhouse. My aunt shared her husband's lust for money — for certainly, one cannot call a feeling so barren, a "passion" — and the victory of half a penny over the grocer, was the only joy that could make her smile.

When I reached the house, I stood long in front of it. It seemed to me that the house looked like a giant mouse trap, and I did not want to go in.

"Jim! Jim!" My aunt was calling me. I saw her face dimly behind the dirty panes of a second story window. The second floor flat was where my uncle and aunt lived; the rest of the house was let to anyone who would pay the rent.

"I am glad I am going to sea. I am glad I am going

to sea." I had said the words aloud to comfort myself. In truth, I feared Captain Mathews, and going to sea had cost my father his life; I did not expect ever to return to port again. Until my mother's death, I had lived in Keynsham. There the Avon is a narrow river and there is no harbor for great ships.

"The grocer, Mr. Jones, would like you to do some errands for him." My aunt did not like to look at me while she spoke, for she did not want me to guess what I already knew; namely, that the grocer paid her for hiring me out to him, while I received only a farthing or two in tips.

I put my bag down in the small entrance hall. My aunt looked at it and frowned.

"I am going to sea," I said. "Tonight on the *Four Winds*. It is a brig." The word sounded strange; and I realized that I did not even know what a brig was.

"Well, run along and do the errands, and I shall cook you a fish for tea." This was a great favor on my aunt's part, for usually only Mr. Pond had anything besides bread for evening tea.

By the time I had returned from doing the last errand for Mr. Jones, I was tired but not unhappy. Mr. Jones was a good-tempered man, for whom I did not mind working. When he heard that I was to sail that night, he gave me a penny; and his wife, a fat woman, who had often been kind to me, gave me a sweet roll and twopence from her own money, which she kept in a box on a shelf in the kitchen. Besides, I had earned two farthings in tips.

"Gluttony, Jim, is a sin. It is almost like stealing, for you are digesting food that you do not need." My uncle looked sternly at me. There had been two fish for tea: one he had eaten, and the other I had shared with my aunt. "Especially in the young," my uncle continued, while my aunt poured him a second cup of tea. "You must learn not to overindulge in the matter of food; for indulgence and ambition are opposite poles, like the North and South Poles of the earth . . . Jim!"

I was startled, for I was wondering what "indulgence" might be.

"Jim, are you ambitious?"

As always in conversations with my uncle, I replied in accordance with what I assumed my uncle wanted me to answer. "Yes," I said timidly.

"In moderation, my boy, ambition is a virtue; in excess it is a vice."

"Like salt," I said without thinking.

"More like pepper, my lad." And my uncle laughed, though no man who did not know him would have recognized that curious sound as anything but a snort: a kind of mixture of a sneeze and a cough.

"Your first trip will be to America, a country inhabited by Indians and thieves. Don't leave the ship, nothing good will ever come out of that country."

I nodded. I was trying to imagine from whom the thieves might steal, if it was not from the Indians, which seemed most unlikely, as — according to what

I had been told — the American Indians were savages. I was also wondering whether there would be any Indians in the town to which the *Four Winds* was sailing.

My uncle's hatred of America stemmed from the fact that a ship, of which he was part owner, had failed to arrive back in Bristol after a voyage to a town called Boston, which is in America. How the Americans could be made responsible for the storm that sunk the topsailed schooner *Lucky Ann* and drowned its crew, I did not understand. But then, there was so little of what my uncle said and thought that I understood.

My aunt, on the other hand, was plainspoken. She did not use long and difficult words. "The blanket . . . Doesn't the captain have to give bedding to his crew?"

My uncle looked at her with surprise.

"I looked in the boy's bag," she explained. "There is a new blanket in it."

"A seaman," my uncle began, and then paused for several seconds. "A seaman has to bring his own bedding, but an old blanket will keep a man as warm as a new one. The quality of warmth to be derived from a blanket is not proportional to its newness."

I did not understand all the words, but the meaning was clear to me: the new blanket that Mr. Hawkins had included in my kit would now warm my uncle. Even though I knew it would be useless to protest, I said, "But it is my blanket. You will get the two pounds from Captain Mathews."

The silence that followed my words was like the silence I later, as a seaman, learned to fear: the silence in the center of a storm.

"Ingratitude." My uncle spoke the word slowly, as if he were tasting it, and finding the taste to be pleasant, he repeated it. "Ingratitude is a sin not only against the persons towards whom it is directed, but against God!"

I bowed my head, not because his scolding hurt me but because I felt tears of anger coming into my eyes. "He must not talk about my mother," I whispered under my breath, knowing all the time that my uncle would.

"Your mother, my wife's sister, harvested the barren crop of ingratitude. Let her life be a lesson to you!"

I knotted my hands under the table. "My mother was good!" I screamed at my uncle.

"The apple falls not far from the trunk of the tree," my aunt remarked.

My uncle added, "Pride goeth before a fall . . . America will suit the lad . . . Thieves and Indians . . ."

It was May and the sun took long to set. When the sky had darkened, my uncle marched me down to the old harbor. Five ships were lying at anchor in the Avon; my uncle pointed to a two-masted one. "That is the *Four Winds*."

My uncle ordered an old man, who made his living by taking seamen out to their ships, to row us out to the *Four Winds*.

"Is it a good ship?" my uncle asked the man, when we were under way.

"Aye, sir," he replied, turning his head a little, so that he could look at it.

"Have you ever been in America?" my uncle inquired.

"No, sir. Never been away from Bristol. The sea doesn't agree with me."

My uncle snorted with disgust, though he, himself, had only once been on a journey, and that had been to London by coach.

As our little boat glided alongside the hull of the *Four Winds*, the ship appeared dark and forbidding. There was an oil lamp in the rigging beside the gangway, from which a rope ladder hung down. To my surprise, my uncle climbed the ladder as agilely as a monkey; but I should have remembered that he went often aboard ships. I followed him up, clutching the rope as I climbed. I did not dare to try to carry my duffel bag with me. When my uncle saw me without my baggage, he screamed down to the old man, "Bring the lad's bag on board, and wait for me!"

The ship was dark and still. In the shadow of the large cabin aft, I saw something move. "What was that?" I whispered.

"What?" My uncle was annoyed with me.

"Over there, among the shadows, I saw something moving."

"Rats, probably," my uncle replied and walked aft. Quickly I caught up with him, for I had always been afraid of rats.

"Ahoy! Who is there?" The voice came from the bow.

"Captain Mathews?" my uncle called back.

I heard deep laughter, which sounded friendly. "The *capitan* is not aboard. He hasn't been aboard for two days, but he'll come tomorrow."

The man who had spoken was a big man. As we approached him, even in the darkness, I could see that he was a head taller than my uncle. He spoke English well, but with a strange accent; and he had not said "captain" but "capitan." Later I learned that he was a Norwegian but he had sailed for many years on Spanish ships.

"Captain Mathews has hired this lad to sail as deck boy. I am the boy's . . . the boy's . . ." My uncle paused and looked away from me. "I am the boy's guardian, and the captain said he would meet me on board."

"The capitan likes to drink. There are many taverns in Bristol." My uncle did not seem willing to converse, so the man turned to me and asked, "What is your name, boy?"

"Jim," I answered and then tried to meet his gaze, for my mother had told me that if you look into a

good man's eyes, he will look back at you, while a bad one will look away.

"Rolf," the stranger said. "My name is Rolf and I am cook aboard." Rolf looked back at me as seriously as I had glanced at him, and then he grinned as though he was laughing at both me and himself.

"You would not know in which establishment I might find Captain Mathews?"

I had all but forgotten my uncle, and it surprised me to hear him speak.

"You might try the Hangman's Folly," Rolf answered. The cook had not said "sir" to my uncle as the ferryman had done, and it pleased me.

"Well, I shall leave the boy to you, then." My uncle started towards the gangway; and Rolf and I followed him.

Next to the bulwarks stood my duffel bag. It looks small and skimpy, I thought. My aunt has taken the blanket.

"Remember to do your duty. An Englishman always does his duty, and leaves impertinence to foreigners."

This was my uncle's parting remark. He even forgot to bid me good-bye; and the words he had spoken had been said for Rolf's sake, more than for mine.

As soon as we could no longer hear the splashing from the oars of the small boat as they hit the water, Rolf led me forward. The ladder down to the forecastle was steep. Since the big room was only lighted by a small oil lamp, it was gloomy. Rolf looked around, then he pointed to a bunk.

"You can take that one, Jim — though God knows if you can keep it, when the rest of the crew comes aboard."

"Do you know the others?" I asked.

"Not a living soul of them; but we'll get to know each other," he said and laughed.

I threw my bag onto the bunk; then I untied it to see what my aunt's long fingers had removed. Just as I had thought, the blanket was gone.

"My aunt," I stammered. "My aunt has stolen my blanket."

Once more Rolf laughed, but not meanly. "I have two blankets. You shall have one of mine, and when you get your hire, you can buy a new one."

In the middle of the cabin was a large wooden table, with wooden benches around it. Rolf sat down across from me.

"But, sir, my uncle will get my hire," I began. Soon I was telling the bitter story of the last two months: those long weeks since my mother's death. The tale pressed through my lips like the spring river that comes from melted snow.

When I had finished Rolf looked at me thoughtfully. "A fish does not need a mama; but a man is not a fish. Yet the sailor is almost a fish, for he, too, has no mama or papa, nor anyone to cry when he is drowned. All sailors are orphans, and that is why the men on shore don't like them."

I was weary, the day had been long. "Doesn't anyone care for sailors?"

Again Rolf laughed, but not as loud as before. He walked over to a small wooden chest, opened it, and took out a blanket. "Here, little sailor, you are tired. Climb into your bunk and sleep."

I took off my new canvas shoes, put them at the bottom of my bunk; then I lay down and wrapped myself in my blanket.

"You didn't answer me; doesn't anyone care for sailors?"

Rolf sighed. "Yes, in every harbor there are men and women who care for sailors . . . care for their brass."

"I don't mean that. Everyone cares for money. My uncle cares a lot, and so does my aunt."

The oil lamp was burning low. Rolf had climbed into the bunk above his chest, and I could not see him.

"The wind, little sailor. The wind cares for us. It is our mama. We are orphans of the wind."

I wanted to ask what he meant, for how could the wind care for anyone? But sleep had crept out of the warm blanket and closed my eyes.

The Crew of the *Four Winds*

3

"GET OUT of that bunk!"

I was still far away in a dream, and the hoarse voice shouting at me seemed to be part of it.

"Get out!"

This time I opened my eyes. Through the skylight came the grey light of morning. I was staring into a face that seemed to me more like a devil's than a human being's.

"Let the boy be."

I sat up. The cabin was filled with sailors. I looked pleadingly at the man who had just spoken. He had turned away, but the sight of his broad back gave me enough courage to look again at the man who was demanding my bunk. He was middling of height and slightly built; but of all his appearance, it was only his face one noticed. In a brawl once — he claimed, himself, that it was in China — someone had cut his face with a knife; and the scars had disfigured him, made of his features a mask. His mouth was drawn down on the right side in a permanent sneer, and from its corner a large, broad scar rose to his eye, causing it to appear slanted and deformed.

"Get out of that bunk!"

I jumped to the deck of the cabin. The man took

my blanket and threw it across the forecastle. My new knife that had been wrapped in the blanket fell with a clatter on the deck. The man picked it up, looked at it, and stuck it into his own belt. At the sight of my knife in another man's belt, my fear left me, and I shouted, "It is mine!"

He grinned and said, "Where did you steal that knife, boy?"

"I didn't steal it! It was given to me." My glance remained fixed upon the knife stuck in the broad leather belt.

"Likely story . . . Someone giving you a knife worth ten bob."

"Mr. Hawkins, where I bought my sea clothes, gave it to me." At these words, some of the men started to laugh, and the man with the scarred face looked about himself with pride.

"The lad has found a place where they give you ten bob, when you buy for two quid."

I shook my head and whispered, "It is my knife."

"Give the boy back his knife." I had not noticed that Rolf had come down the ladder. Standing at the bottom, he glared at my tormentor with an expression of contempt on his face. The men moved away from the center of the cabin, leaving space for a fight.

"Give the lad back his knife, Shanghai." This time it was the broadly built older man who again came to my defense.

Shanghai looked around the forecastle; then after

removing my knife from the sheath, he balanced it in his hand. "Stand still, boy," he said.

I stood perfectly motionless, my back against the wall at the far end of the cabin.

"If you move, I might clip your ear . . . or cut it off."

"No," I whispered. I had no sooner pronounced the word then I heard the knife hit the board beside my head. I turned. The knife was embedded in the wood, less than an inch away from my ear.

"Is this a circus performance?" The voice boomed loud and angry through the forecastle, and everyone turned to look at the speaker. He was a small man, almost as square as he was tall. He had pale blue eyes, that seemed fit to mirror neither love nor hate, but only scorn. "I am Mr. Crane. I am first mate on this ship. You don't know me now; but any man among you who won't work or causes trouble, on this voyage, will never forget my name." Mr. Crane looked from one to the other of us, as if he did not want merely to scrutinize each face, but see into every soul, as well.

"We are sailors, not criminals, sir." The old man who had twice defended me stepped forward. He had a full beard which was yellow about the mouth from tobacco.

"Any man can call himself a sailor, when he is sail-ing an ocean of beer in a tavern." Mr. Crane paused, looked at the older man, then nodded his head as if he were answering a question, and started to climb up the ladder. Halfway up, he turned. "We are sailing with the tide tonight. Change your shore clothes and come up on deck."

As soon as the first mate had gone, the men started to grumble among themselves about Mr. Crane. "He is a devil, he is!" said a lanky youth, whose face was pitted with the marks of the pox.

I picked up my blanket and my duffel bag, which were lying on the deck, and began my search for an empty bunk. I was frightened of Shanghai and the other men, so I looked for the worst bunk I could find. Rolf drew my knife out of the plank, took my duffel bag from me and threw it into a bunk far forward. It was the coldest and dampest bunk in the forecastle, and many a time would I lie there shivering, listening to the thunder of the waves breaking against the bow of the ship. Shanghai must have felt this as a victory, for he threw the sheath to my knife after me. I put my knife in my belt, and following Rolf, I climbed the ladder.

This was the first time I saw the *Four Winds* in daylight. The masts were immeasurably high. They were swaying gently, while the deck seemed completely still. Rolf looked with disgust up at the masts and said, "Full-rigged, she is; but foul-rigged is what I would call her. Come along, Jim." He led me to a small cabin, right behind the foremast, and pushed me through the door. When he had closed it behind me, he said, "This is my kingdom."

I smiled. If this were a kingdom, then it must be one of the smaller ones. In the fore section there were a cooking range and a table, which took up so much of the floor space that what remained of the deck was only an alleyway. In the aft part, a large box ran from wall to wall. The top of it was used by the cook and his visitors as a bench; the box was a storage place for coal, the fuel of the stove.

"Whenever the sea gets too rough, you can steer for port here."

I nodded gratefully. Without asking me whether I wanted it, Rolf poured some tea into a mug and passed it to me; then he offered me two ship's biscuits. The biscuits were dry and hard.

"The man who wanted my bunk, is his name really Shanghai?"

Rolf dunked a biscuit into his warm tea while he spoke. "Most men who go to sea — at least those who take berth on a brig like the *Four Winds* — leave their names ashore. The capitan does not ask your name. All he wants are two strong hands and a belly that doesn't ache when it is fed on rusty nails instead of food. The capitan has a name because he has to sign for the goods we need. Mr. Crane has a name because one day he will be a capitan, if he leaves the brandy alone. A sailor, Jim, doesn't need a name. You can call him Shanghai or Puddin'head or Porridge, as some say Nelson's cook was called. It's all the same. Now the old man with a beard is called Noah. It may be what his mother called him and it may not; but Noah it will be as long as he's on this ship, no matter what the church register says."

I nodded, wondering what my name would be. I had always been called Jim, though my Christian name was James. "What will they call me?" I asked.

Rolf laughed. "I should think that 'boy' would be a very good name for you. 'Jim' is short and handy, too; it won't waste too much of a man's breath. My name is Rolf, and Rolf I am called." Rolf suddenly became almost solemn. "But it would be wise, Jim, for you to say 'sir' to old Noah, for he has taken a liking to you, and a boy on his first voyage needs friends. When the capitan is in a mean temper, because the wind has blown down his royals, he will let the mates feel it; they, in turn, will curse the sailors; and the sailors, according to age and ability, will curse each other; then the youngest man will kick the boy."

I hoped that the "royals" — whatever they were — would not blow down too often. "What does the boy do?" I asked.

"There's an old tomcat lurking around the ship. You could find it and pull its tail."

I laughed because I was so fond of cats I could not imagine pulling Mr. Tom's tail.

I heard a loud whistle, coming from outside. I must have appeared very startled, for Rolf explained, "The bosun's whistle. You'll get as used to that as you will to the sound of a bell." Quickly Rolf put away the mugs and motioned for me to follow him.

Once out in the daylight, I realized how dim the light had been in the cookhouse; yet this had seemed almost bright compared to the twilight of the forecastle. On the larboard side, by the main hatch, all the crew were assembled. Aft near the cabin stood Captain Mathews, the First Mate Crane, and a third man, who was younger but taller and thinner than Mr. Crane. The three men acted as if they thought they were alone, and did not as much as glance at the rest of us. The bosun, an elderly man with white hair and not a tooth in his mouth, looked at the officers nervously, and then looked out over the railing.

"Is there any grog on board?" the young man with the pitted face asked the bosun.

The bosun did not reply, but gazed into the young man's eyes until his poor face turned red.

"A ship without grog is like hell without fire and brimstone. There will be enough of it for you to lose your soul." Some of the men laughed, but uncomfortably, for none of them was certain that old Noah was not in earnest.

Those of the men who knew each other stood in groups; the others stood alone, trying to put on an air of not caring that they were friendless. Shanghai was standing with two other young men. The youth who had asked about the grog approached them; but Shanghai turned his back, and his two friends at once did the same. A moment later, the young man pushed me as he went by, and said scornfully, "Get out of my way, boy!"

As I quickly stepped aside, I thought, the captain does not need to lose his royals for Jim to get into trouble. Then, as luck would have it, I noticed a large tomcat, his face scarred and his ears torn, passing along the side of the railing. He was walking briskly aft, as if he had an important message for the captain. "I shan't kick you," I whispered to myself, "but maybe, I shall make a friend of you."

"Men," Mr. Crane began, "Mr. Goodfellow, here, is second mate; he'll take the larboard watch. I will take the starboard. The bosun will be on larboard watch, the carpenter on the starboard. As I call out each name, the man called will step over on the starboard side, he will belong to my watch. The remainder will be on Mr. Goodfellow's."

Now the officer of the watch is the king of the watch, for a ship, even a merchant ship is a kingdom not a republic. All the men looked at Mr. Goodfellow, trying to judge what kind of captain of the watch he would be; but that gentleman looked out at the shore, as if the business at hand held no interest for him. Still, I believe that if it had been up to the sailors to choose, then the larboard watch would have mustered all the men, and Mr. Crane would have worked a lonely starboard watch. But seamen make only one choice: the signing of the ship's roll; from then on, they are as choiceless as a farm horse. I myself had only one wish: not to be on the same watch as Shanghai; so when, as last man, I was called to walk to the starboard side, I breathed freer seeing Shanghai still standing by the larboard railing.

Noah was among the men of my watch, for he was the ship's carpenter. What pleased me less was that the youth who had pushed me was also my watch mate. Someone was talking to him and calling him, "Pimples."

It was the middle of the morning, and half of the morning watch, which runs from eight to noon, had already passed. Starboard was on duty. As I had feared I would be, I was set to work with Pimples. We were to polish the brass work on the aft cabin, which was greyish green with dirt.

My companion had smiled when the other men called him Pimples; but there had been as much merriment in his smile as there is joy in the wagging tail of a beaten dog.

"What is your name?" I asked.

He looked suspiciously at me, then over his shoulder to see if anyone was watching us. Finally, he answered in a whisper, "Tom Neal."

"Tom, Tom the piper's son . . ." The nursery rhyme ran round in my head, and I wondered how many times it had been shouted after Tom Neal.

"Put some knuckle grease into your work!"

Tom was shouting at me. Confused, I stopped working and looked about the deck. Mr. Crane had just walked past us, but in spite of Tom's remark, he had not even bothered to give us a glance.

I began to rub the brass again, as I thought angrily, "All right, 'Pimples' you be." Silently, side by side, we worked for the rest of the watch.

Weighing Anchor

4

"Rat soup," one of the men remarked, and sniffed with disgust at the pot of food I had carried from the cookhouse down to the forecastle. It was a heavy iron pot, and I lifted it with difficulty to the table. The men of my watch were all sitting on the benches around the table; each had a plate and a fork or a spoon in front of him. Some of the men never used forks, finding that a knife could do a fork's work, while a spoon was handy for the gravy.

Captain Mathews, who was part owner of the ship, was as stingy as my uncle, and the *Four Winds* had never sailed, under him, with a full crew. There were neither cabin boys nor a cook's boy on board. Each man took care of his own plate and cutlery; and the younger members of the crew, besides doing their regular work, had to be messboys. There were four boys on board: two on each watch. Pimples, who was sixteen, was the oldest; he had only one journey on a barque to his credit, and was not counted for much among the other sailors. One of the boys on larboard watch was called Fatty, because he was so obese; the other, like myself, was allowed to keep his own name, probably because it was so short: he was called Jack. Fatty had been an orphan from birth and had been brought up in the Poor House. There he had learned that what old Parson Perkins thundered out over the bent heads of the congregation in the chapel in Bristol, on Sundays, was only too true: The purpose of this life is suffering. A cuff or a cursing, even a beating Fatty bore in meekness, like a tree on a windswept coast; but a soft voice made him suspicious, and an act of kindness could arouse his contempt. Jack was different. Average of height and more than average of strength, he was ever ready to fight for his rights. He carried himself with an air of independence that, though it annoyed some of the older men, won him many friends.

"The Good Lord starved in the desert," Noah the carpenter remarked and looked reprovingly at the sailor who had complained about our dinner. This sailor was called Squinty, because his eyes always looked as if he were staring into the sun.

"The Lord suffered for the sins of the world, we will suffer for the sake of Captain Mathews' cash box," explained Keith the foretopman. Keith had once been captain of the foretop in one of Her Majesty's frigates. He was tall and slender and carried himself with a gentle air. Keith, the bosun, Noah, and the cook were the only really able seamen aboard the *Four Winds*.

Old Noah took another spoonful of the stew, after chewing and swallowing it carefully, he said, "Let the sinners be consumed out of the earth, and let the wicked be no more."

Those who, like myself, did not know old Noah looked at him with astonishment, for what he had said did not seem to make any sense. Later we were to grow used to hearing old Noah's quotations. As the whale had swallowed Jonah, the carpenter had swallowed the Bible; and as Jonah had stayed hale and hearty inside the whale, so each page of the Good Book was intact inside old Noah. Seldom did the words of the Bible that came from the carpenter's lips make much sense. It was as if all the sentences of the Bible had been imprisoned inside him, and when he opened his mouth, those nearest to his throat jumped out.

Keith the foretopman only laughed, and ladled some more stew onto his plate. "Jim, here, will be lonesome, being the only man left to man the ship."

All the men turned towards me and I looked down at my plate, as my face grew red. They were all laughing, but one of them said, "An angel doesn't carry a knife."

Starboard watch would have been free in the afternoon, but so much work needed to be done before we could get underway, that both watches were on duty. As I hardly knew the difference between the foremast and the mainmast, I was ordered to help Rolf with the carrying of the food supplies to the storeroom below the quarterdeck cabin.

I was carrying a sack of potatoes below, when the door to the captain's cabin opened and the Captain looked out at me. "Is it heavy?" he grumbled.

Rolf had placed the sack on my back; it weighed fifty pounds and I could not have lifted it myself. Slowly I nodded my head.

"We'll make a man of you or feed you to the sharks," he said and then laughed loudly. He closed the door to his cabin, and the next time that anyone saw him we were ready to weigh anchor.

"He is the same sort as my uncle," I thought, as I trudged to the ladder which led to the storeroom.

When we had finished carrying the stores below, Rolf took me aft to the wheelhouse. We stood by the railing and looked out towards the shore. Rolf stopped his pipe and lighted it. "Jim, look at the land and remember what you see, you'll be a full grown man, perhaps, before you see Bristol again."

I glanced towards land, but such were my memories of the past few months that I did not care when I next saw Bristol. "Rolf," I asked hesitantly, "what are the 'royals?'"

The cook laughed. "They are the sails at the top of the mast, below them are the topgallant sails; then come the upper and lower topsails; below these, nearest to the deck are the biggest sails, called the mainsail. The *Four Winds* is called full-rigged because she carries all the sails on both her masts." The cook pointed to a great boom, just above us; a sail was furled to it. "That is the main trysail. Out by the bowsprit, you will find the flying jib and the foretopmast staysail, and, Jim . . ." Rolf lowered his voice. "If this were an honest ship, then every one of those sails

would be used to cover the hold."

"Why?" I whispered, for surely a ship was not like a person and could not be honest or dishonest.

"Those sails are rotten," he replied.

We had caught Mr. Crane's eye and he screamed at us to get forward. Though Mr. Crane had sworn, Rolf took the time to knock out his pipe against the railing and shove it in his jacket before he started forward.

"Jim, the aft part of the ship — aft of the mainmast — is called the quarterdeck; it is the land of the officers, as the forecastle is the country of the men. Don't ever go aft, unless you are ordered to; for the sight of a sailor on the quarterdeck makes an officer as mad as an Irishman, when he sees an Englishman in the streets of Dublin."

"Boy!" It was Mr. Goodfellow calling me. "Climb up to the fore-topmast crosstree with this." The mate slung a large, heavy coil of rope at me. So confused was I that I looked at the mainmast, but Rolf, who was still standing at my side, threw the coil over one of my shoulders and pulled me in the direction of the foremast rigging.

Pointing high above to a man who seemed almost to be standing on the side of the mast, he said, "Climb up and give it to him."

I climbed quickly, not looking down before I came to the foretop. The mast of the ship is made in three pieces. The foretop is just above the big boom that holds outstretched the mainsail. At the foretop ends the first part of the mast, and here there is a platform where it is pleasant to sit in fair weather. The rigging narrows as it goes up to the fore-topmast crosstree, where the second part of the mast ends. Above it, is the slender topgallant mast. Beyond the foretop, I grasped the rigging even tighter. When at last I came to the crosstree, the man there took the rope from me and laughed.

"Look down, boy."

I did as I was told. I felt faint, for the ship seemed so small; and for a moment, I feared that I would let go of the rigging. I turned my glance upward again and looked into the face of Shanghai; he was grinning. His foot stepped onto my left hand and slowly he pressed his weight down on it. I didn't cry out, but kept staring into his face. With a final laugh, he took his foot away and started climbing up the rigging above me. I went down slowly, feeling my way with my feet until I reached the foretop; then I stopped and looked below. "I am not going to be scared," I said aloud to myself; and when I saw Rolf, who was standing by the cookhouse, wave to me, I waved back and laughed.

The sun had set when we got under way, and the lanterns had been lighted. The tide was fair for us, as was the wind, which was blowing gently from the east. All the younger seamen were in the rigging, letting go the sails; while the rest of us were manning the capstan.

"Up anchor!" screamed Mr. Crane.

We started to walk around, pushing the capstan bars. I thought of an old blind horse that I had once seen walking round and round in a horse mill.

"Let go upper and lower topsails!" screamed the mate.

I looked aloft; the big sails were being filled by the evening breeze, and the *Four Winds* heeled over.

"Anchor up!" shouted the carpenter. The anchor hit the bow of the ship with a hollow sound.

"Come on, my hearties, fall to . . . fall to . . . Man the braces."

Not knowing what the orders meant, I followed the other men about and pulled on the ropes that they pulled on. Soon all sails were set; the anchor secured; and the thousand other things which have to be done almost at the same moment, when a ship gets under-way, were performed.

Looking up at the great mass of sails, I felt proud; and I realized that, though a sailor is reckoned as less than a dog by those who own a door that can be secured at night with an iron bolt, he is — among all the slaves of mankind — the nearest to being a free man.

"Larboard watch can go below."

I was disappointed, because I was tired; still, I suppose I would have lingered above, even if it had not been my watch; for, though Bristol meant only pain to me, beyond it there was a town with gardens and trees growing at the Avon's edge, where I had lived with my mother.

"May I have the boy?"

I turned around. It was Rolf. Mr. Crane merely nodded. He did not even ask what work the cook, who was not on deck duty, might want me for. Rolf belonged to no watch and was only concerned with the sailing of the ship when the order "All men ahoy!" was called.

When we reached the cookhouse, Rolf motioned towards the bench and handed me a mug of steaming tea. Laughing, he said, "You are a lucky boy, Jim. The captain may be God or the devil, all according to his inclination; but a sailor who has the cook for a friend can always get his clothes dry and have a drink of witch-water to warm his inside with."

Aye, Jim, I thought, better to be a sailor and eat rat soup than be a man like my uncle, sitting in an office, counting other men's gold.

Under Sail

5

THREE DAYS OUT OF BRISTOL the *Four Winds* ran into a gale. It was blowing from the northeast, and for two days the ship ran before it, whipped by the winds as a horse is whipped by an angry rider. What Rolf had said about the sails proved true: both royals and one of the topgallant sails blew away in the first gust of the storm. When the gale hit us, Mr. Goodfellow and the larboard watch were on deck. I was awakened by the hoarse cry of "All men on deck! Ahoy, all men on deck! Save ship! Save ship!"

The starboard watch tumbled out of their bunks. It was during the dogwatch, and the cabin was lit by the drowsy, little oil lamp. When we got on deck the wind hit our faces and the sound of the wind deafened our ears.

"Come on, my hearties, save sail!" I heard Mr. Crane's voice above the wind. "Down the topsail. Come on! Come on!"

For a moment I thought of climbing the rigging; but as I came near the railing, a sea broke in over the side and knocked my feet from under me. When I regained my balance, I saw some of the men taking down the foresails, and I ran to help them. The canvas was wet and stiff.

"Down the flying jib! Come on, hearties." The voice came from near by.

"Save the flying jib!" Mr. Goodfellow pushed the man next to me and myself towards the bow of the ship. The older seaman, without looking to see who his companion was, jumped over the bow, and holding onto the bowsprit worked his way out to the tip of it and the flying jib, which was slowly being lowered.

With my feet on the jib footrope and my arms around the bowsprit, I worked my way out. Each time the ship ran down the waves, I was covered by

water and foam; and each time it climbed, I seemed to be thrown right into the sky. How we got the flying jib tied under, I hardly remember, for all the while we were out there, I felt certain that the next wave would grab me in its arms and bury me forever in the sea.

When all the sails had been made fast, the *Four Winds* was tearing along, carrying only two reefed topsails and the jib. Three sails had been lost; the torn pieces that were left would serve only as paint rags. Still, we could count ourselves lucky that the topgallant masts had not blown away with the sails.

The *Four Winds* had been carrying all sails when the starboard watch had gone below. Though the wind had been blowing freshly, Captain Mathews had not allowed Mr. Crane to make fast the royals and the topgallant sails before his watch was over. Mr. Goodfellow, though not an incapable officer, had one glaring fault — common enough, unfortunately: he was afraid of his superior officers. This fear kept him from calling the captain or giving orders for taking down of sails before it was too late. Captain Mathews was a hard master, not only to the crew but to the officers as well, and he would readily call a prudent man a coward. For fear of the captain's tongue, the ship was nearly lost; and we came close to giving up the only thing a poor jack tar owns: our lives.

When everything was tidy, starboard watch was allowed to go below; but only half an hour remained of the larboard watch, and though the men took off their oilcloths and lay down on their bunks, none tried to sleep.

"The voice of the Lord is upon the waters," declared the old carpenter, as the boards of his bunk groaned under his weight.

Although the men often made light of old Noah's remarks, they were more superstitious than religious, and they would wait for fair weather before making the carpenter a butt of their jokes.

"We should have heaved to," Keith the foretopman said. "A storm likes a fighter better than a coward."

Keith's bunk was not far from mine, and he had been kind to me, so I mustered up the courage to ask why. Keith — half annoyed and half flattered — said, "Ahoy there, and what did the boy do?"

With a bit of pride in my voice, I answered, "I tucked in the flying jib."

"Aye, and so he did, and cheated the sharks this time," added the sailor who had been my partner at the work.

The words felt warm. Wet and cold as I was, I silently blessed the man for saying them.

"We shall make a sailor of him," said Keith the foretopman, but he did not answer my question. I quickly learned not to ask any questions while any of the other men was within earshot, for though Keith, Noah, or Rolf would willingly answer if I was alone, they felt ashamed of talking to a boy when their comrades were present. The next day Keith explained, while we stood alone beside the rail, both of us gazing at the horizon, why he had wanted the ship steered into the storm rather than running away from it. The bow is the strongest part of the ship, constructed to stand the fist of the sea, while the stern in the weakest part. When you run in front of a storm, the stern receives a battering it was not built to withstand, and often the rudder is smashed. A rudderless ship in a storm is soon a mastless hull.

On the morning of the third day, after the gale had begun, the winds grew weak and changing; we let out reefs and set new sails. The sea, however, was still rough, and the ship rolled from side to side, as it slid up and down the waves. Many of the men who had not been seasick during the storm now felt their stomachs rebelling against them. I had a touch of it in the morning, but by noon I was hale and hearty enough to joke about it with Rolf, for I was looking forward to my dinner.

There was one man aboard who was so miserably sick that I had to perform his duties. He was Captain Mathews' steward; a member of the crew that I had not happened onto till now, because he did not berth in the forecastle but slept in a bunk aft in the storage room. His name was William Jones; but as far as the crew of the *Four Winds* were concerned, the parson could have saved himself the trouble of baptizing him, for he was never called any other name than "The Rat." A sailor will pay a certain amount of respect to his officers, much as a commoner will pay to the Queen, but for such men as the steward William

Jones he feels only contempt; for The Rat was the captain's lackey, as the policeman is the Queen's.

The captain's steward alone had no home aboard the *Four Winds*. The forecastle was barred to him; on the quarterdeck he was a servant; and being afraid of heights he could not climb the foretop. The only place he could call his own was the airless storeroom, filled with the smell of hemp and tar. Even Potiphar, the ship's cat, had better holes to hide in, and should the cat care to enter the forecastle, it was a welcome guest.

The officers ate in their cabins. Though a common room was at their disposal, they only used it when they were in port. It was The Rat's duty to carry the meals from the cookhouse and serve them to the officers. When the steward was sick, the honor of performing his duties fell on one of the boys. During the worst of the storm, the job had been easy, for only biscuits and cold salt beef were everyone's fare. The only cooking done in a heavy sea is the making of tea. But now that the winds had lost their force, the captain ordered hot food made for the noonday meal. Rolf cooked his usual rat soup: a kind of stew made from potatoes, onions, and salt beef. For the officers, however, a hen, which had been half drowned by the gale, was cooked. Potiphar and the innumerable rats were not the only animals aboard the *Four Winds*. Next to the cookhouse was a hen's coop, containing twelve bedraggled hens and a cock, who crowed in the morning proudly, as though he knew he was a sailor. The member of the cock's harem to be served

to the officers was an elderly lady, who had no tail-feathers; and I heard one of the crew say that he was convinced that her first berth had been aboard Captain Noah's ark.

The boiled hen was portioned according to rank: Captain Mathews received the white meat; the first mate, Mr. Crane, all the dark meat except for one drumstick; Mr. Goodfellow was given the wings, the innards, and one drumstick. Mr. Goodfellow was served first, for he was going on watch; then Mr. Crane; and last the captain, the king of our wooden world. Neither Mr. Goodfellow nor Mr. Crane had talked to me when I brought them their food, and merely nodded by way of saying thank you.

When I entered the captain's cabin, I found Captain Mathews studying some charts that were spread out over the table. I looked unhappily at the charts, wondering where I ought to put down the plate, not daring to ask the captain. Suddenly Mr. Mathews turned around and grunted annoyedly. Hastily he rolled up the charts and put them on his bunk. Immediately, I placed the plate on the table; but such was the movement of the ship, that had I let go of it, it would have fallen to the deck. The captain laughed at the sight of me standing there, keeping myself as far away as I could from his table, while still grasping his dinner plate. Finally, he took hold of it himself and pointed to a drawer. In it I found a linen napkin, a knife, a fork, spoons, and a silver drinking cup. I took a large napkin and spread it out on the table; the captain deigned to help me by lifting his plate. On one side of the plate I put a knife and on the other a fork. The captain snorted, while he reversed the cutlery, which I had put down incorrectly.

"The cup."

Gingerly, I put the silver cup beside his plate. The captain motioned towards the cupboard. "Open it." The cupboard was filled with bottles, which all, except for the one that was open, were lying securely, each in its tiny wooden cradle. The opened bottle was held upright by two ropes.

I poured the wine, and Captain Mathews quickly

drank half a cup, and nodded, which I rightly supposed meant that he wished me to fill the cup once
more.

"Put the bottle back now, boy."

I hoped that my duties in the captain's cabin were
at an end; but I was not dismissed. I sensed that it
pleased the captain to see me standing there frightened; and all at once, I felt sorry for The Rat, realizing what he had to experience every day. I had heard
it said that the steward hated everyone else aboard,
and now I thought I understood why, though I could
not have expressed it in words.

"Are the men satisfied?" the captain asked, and
then continued chewing carefully the final piece of
hen.

My head bobbed up and down.

"Speak up, boy."

"Yes," I muttered, knowing that a lie would serve
me better than the truth, which was that none of the
men was satisfied either with the captain or his ship.

"A bunch of ill-mannered cutthroats — criminals
all."

I was avoiding the captain's gaze, and in doing
so, I glanced at the rolled-up charts that lay on the
bunk.

"Have you ever seen a sea chart before?" Captain
Mathews asked angrily.

"No, sir," I whispered, and looked down at the
deck.

The blow of the captain's hand against my cheek

came as a complete surprise to me; and I cried out, while tears came into my eyes.

"Take the plate away. Wash the cutlery and the cup, and return them at once."

I grabbed the things and ran from the cabin. Climbing up the ladder, I almost collided with Mr. Crane. "I'm sorry, sir," I mumbled and ducked under his arm, out onto the deck.

A few moments later when I returned to the captain's cabin with the cutlery and the silver cup, the captain was again studying his charts, but this time he did not acknowledge either my arrival or my departure.

As it was not my watch, I climbed the rigging to the foretop. I sat up there alone and thought about what had happened: Why had Captain Mathews not liked my looking at the charts? What could it matter, when I understood not a chart, nor did I know where in America that city called Boston, for which the *Four Winds* was sailing, might be.

6

"Eight bells," Mr. Crane called out; and the carpenter who was standing at the wheel, struck the bell at his side eight times.

"Freedom," I thought. But I did not dare stop polishing the brass of the compass house, for I knew that the officers always noticed who was the first person to stop his work when watches were relieved.

"A beautiful Sunday afternoon," Mr. Goodfellow greeted Mr. Crane.

"Yes, Mr. Goodfellow, an afternoon suited for walking in a park with a lass on one's arm." Mr. Crane sighed dramatically, and I suppressed a smile, for I could not imagine Mr. Crane walking arm in arm with a girl.

"The course is southwest by west, and keep her steady." With these words Mr. Crane left us, having cast a glance at the compass.

A seaman from larboard watch now came and stood by the carpenter. As the newcomer grabbed the wheel, Noah called out the course, "Southwest by west."

"Southwest by west," repeated the seaman.

"And keep her steady," added Mr. Goodfellow. Then it struck me that the relieving of a watch reminded me of services in the chapel at home.

I picked up my rags; letting the carpenter go before me, I left the compass house. With his broad shoulders and long white locks of hair, he looked like one of the Prophets in the Old Testament. He was a good seaman and a fine carpenter; yet as certain as I am that he had no enemies aboard, I am sure he had no friends. Again I thought of Jonah; each ship that the carpenter took berth on was a whale that swallowed him up, and like Jonah he sailed the seas as if his voyages only had meaning to God. Had he a wife and children? We knew not. Indeed, we knew nothing about the carpenter. A sailor dreams of land, of harbor; but the carpenter — wasn't it the storm he dreamed of, the whirlpool, the dark bottomless sea beneath the hull?

It was a beautiful evening. The men of starboard watch ate their supper of cold salt beef, biscuits, and tea sweetened with treacle, on the deck. The sun was setting in a purple sea, and a light breeze from south-southeast blew gently against our faces.

"Aye," said Keith the foretopman, "now jack tar is master of the world. Sing us a song, Rolf, but let it be better than your cooking."

Words about his inability as a cook never angered Rolf. He smiled, leaned against the railing, and looking aloft, as if the verses of his song were to be read in the sails, he started to sing.

In Bristol lives my lassie;
Her cheeks are like the rose,

Her lips are like the cherry
That in the summer grows.
Blow winds, blow winds,
To Bristol will I go.

Sweet are the lassies
Under the cross,
Sweet and loving are they,
But my lassie is a Bristol lass.
Blow winds, blow winds,
To Bristol will I go.

The storms blow gay and free
Around the cape of fear.
And many a lad has rested there
Blind his eye and deaf his ear.

The ship ne'er saw port again
Drowned was the lad so fair.
The winds played so lonesome
Upon the empty air.
Blow winds, blow winds,
To Bristol will I go.

In Bristol lives his lassie;
Her cheeks are white as snow.
She is waiting for her laddie
That lies beneath the foam.
Blow winds, blow winds,
To Bristol will I go.

Almost all the songs of sailors are sad; they are often concerned with death, yet it cheers one to hear them sung. I wanted to ask Rolf why this was true, but I did not dare.

"'Don Gonzales' . . . Sing 'Don Gonzales,'" demanded Keith.

Again Rolf looked up at the sky.

> *Don Gonzalez was a pirate,*
> *His ship, it was a brig;*
> *It had only four guns*
> *And rotten was its rig.*
> *Don Gonzalez, Don Gonzalez,*
> *The poor buccaneer.*
>
> *From Tripoli in Barbary*
> *He set his sail so gay,*
> *And hauled up his roger*
> *In the winds to play.*
> *Don Gonzalez, Don Gonzalez*
> *The poor buccaneer.*
>
> *From England came a frigate,*
> *Its sails were full and new;*
> *Its course was towards Barbary.*
> *Blow winds and salten dew.*
> *Don Gonzalez, Don Gonzalez,*
> *The poor buccaneer.*
>
> *"Sail ho!" a pirate called;*
> *"A frigate do I see*
> *With thirty guns loaded;*

From that we cannot flee."
Don Gonzalez, Don Gonzalez,
The poor buccaneer.

The Englishmen their rigging took,
The roger fell on deck.
Don Gonzalez nailed it to the mast
For he would not stretch his neck.
Don Gonzalez, Don Gonzalez,
The poor buccaneer.

And ere the day was over
The pirates all were dead.
Cry will the girls in Tripoli
And lonesome be their bed.
Don Gonzalez, Don Gonzales,
The poor buccaneer.

This song was a favorite among the crew; and their sympathies were always with the pirate, for the Englishmen had thirty guns and poor Don Gonzales only four.

Suddenly a voice shouted from the foretop. "Sail ho! On the starboard bow!"

All of us went to the railing, but we could see nothing. Keith and I climbed the rigging; and from the foretop, we caught a glimpse of a speck on the horizon.

The world outside the lonely ship is like the world the stars must pass through in their course in the heavens. It is only to be observed for signs of tide and wind. A house belongs to the trees in the garden, and the birds will build their nests in its eaves; but the ship does not belong to the sea, except when its hull is a home for the fishes of the deep. When two ships meet at sea, the ocean seems friendlier, and often ships will go hours out of their course for no other purpose than to discover who the other wanderer might be. When you have Cape Horn in front of you, the sight of the barque *Mary Jane* from Bristol, homeward bound, can fill your heart with happiness.

"What ship?" Mr. Goodfellow cried out.

The watchman who had climbed to the very top of the gallantmast called back, "She is full-rigged, sir . . . three-masted."

"What course?" It was the gruff voice of the captain.

"Due south. She is a man-of-war, sir."

The sun had set and the sea was growing dark. "We shan't see nought but her lights, if we see them," Squinty called as we were climbing down.

"Can you still see her?" Captain Mathews shouted up at the man in the rigging.

"Aye, sir. I think she is changing course, sir. More westerly!"

Captain Mathews was perusing the horizon with his telescope.

"She will want to talk to us, that is why she is changing course," Keith said to no one in particular. Everyone was staring into the dusk, still hoping to see the full-rigged man-of-war.

"The *Four Winds* is no race horse," Keith remarked

turning from the railing, "and you won't get sight of the frigate's lanterns before four bells have been struck."

When the foretopman mentioned lanterns, we all looked up at our own and saw with surprise that they had not been lit.

"Bosun," Rolf called, "have you forgotten to fill the lanterns?"

The bosun, who was standing aft, turned his back on us and approached the captain, touching his cap as he did so. Captain Mathews put away his telescope, for it had grown too dark for him to be able to see anything. Taking no notice of the bosun, he called up to the lookout, "Can you still see her?"

From high up the rigging, Blackie shouted down, "No, sir."

Now the captain motioned to Mr. Goodfellow and, still ignoring the bosun, talked with the mate. Together they walked aft to the wheel. Finally Mr. Goodfellow gave an order to the bosun.

The bosun's voice rang out, "All men prepared to go about!"

When a brig or a full-rigged ship goes about, both watches have to work, even if the wind is not stiff. Larboard watch takes care of the foresails; starboard of the mainsails. Soon we heard Mr. Goodfellow cry out from the foremast, "Everything clear, sir!"

We were busy loosening ropes. One of the main braces gave us trouble, and it was a while before Mr. Crane could call, "All clear aft!"

The captain was standing beside the man at the wheel. I did not hear the order, but I saw the wheel being turned, and felt the deck changing under us, as she heaved to.

"Pull, my hearties! Pull!"

The jib and the other foresails were loose. I heard the noise of the wind shaking them; then, as the big sails filled out again, the *Four Winds* leaned over on her larboard side and glided silently through the waters on course northeast by east.

"My God . . . I think he's sailing for Bristol again," one of the men said with astonishment.

As soon as the work of going about was finished, and the last rope drawn tight and fastened, we of the starboard watch were at liberty again; and we collected near the cookhouse to discuss the strange maneuver. The only thing upon which we all agreed was that the man-of-war had been the cause of our changing course.

"A bloody pirate, that is what she is," Shanghai exclaimed, as he passed near us on his way to the forepart of the ship. Most of the men laughed; nonetheless, we began to talk of pirates, who once made the waters around the Leeward Islands their own.

We sailed for two hours on the new course. Just after four bells had been struck, we were called upon to turn the *Four Winds* about again.

"Now we shall pass aft of her, if she has held her course," Keith the foretopman said to me.

"But why? Keith," I asked, "was she a pirate?"

"Pirate!" he snorted, and looked about furtively to see whether anyone was within earshot. Finding no one, he continued, "Have you ever heard of the cargo being aboard and the hatches closed, before the new crew comes aboard?"

I shook my head vigorously, though the fact that the *Four Winds* had been loaded before I came aboard meant nothing to me.

"It is war, my boy!"

"With the French?" I asked excitedly, for in my mind the only nation that England had ever been at war against was the French.

Keith laughed. "The Americans."

I wrinkled my forehead, for the thought that we could be at war with the Indians and the thieves before I had had a chance to see their strange country, disappointed me. "Why should we be at war with them?"

Keith looked at me with disgust. "Jim, my boy, we ain't at war against them; they are at war with each other."

"How can they be?"

Keith spat out over the railing. "Like Cromwell," he muttered; then, probably because he thought this was enough of an answer to offer a boy, he walked from me to join the other men.

I stood long by the larboard railing, looking out over the sea. Once I thought I saw a lantern far away in the distance.

Captain Mathews Makes a Speech

7

WHEN THE SUN ROSE, there was no sign of the man-of-war we had sighted the day before. Only the immeasurable sea met our eyes. So pleasant and warm was the day that where the sea and sky met they melted into one. At first, none of us spoke of what had happened the previous evening, as though no one believed it. It was Pimples who finally mentioned the matter. Pathetic in his self-importance, he started to talk to a group of the older sailors, as if he were a schoolteacher, and they a class of dunces.

"Mind you, Mr. Mathews is going to make a pretty penny on this cargo of ours, if it doesn't blow us all to kingdom come. We ain't sailing for Boston, but a good deal south of there, where a man can buy a pretty slave girl, if he's a mind to."

"And brass enough in his pocket," mumbled one of the other seamen.

Looking straight at Pimples, Rolf said, "Aye, we are going to the land where they sell men. What do you think we could get for this fellow?"

The men laughed. One suggested a dead fish, another an old boot; and there were a few even more derogatory suggestions.

Pimples blushed. "They don't sell white men."

Rolf jumped up and acted as though he was looking for something. "The tar bucket . . . Where is the tar bucket? We shall paint the fellow so black that even his mother will think him pretty, and sell him to the highest bidder."

One of the sailors found a bucket with tar, and Pimples started to run away. The sailor raced after him, but Pimples climbed up the rigging. Everyone except Pimples was very amused; and I admit that I laughed too, though I wondered at the foolishness of the fellow, for Pimples was not as stupid as he was foolish. As some men know instinctively the right thing to say, so Pimples inevitably knew the wrong.

"Aye, the course has been far too south," Squinty muttered. Then he nodded his head, and, by that movement, he meant to tell us that he had guessed the true course of the *Four Winds* when we had weighed anchor in Bristol.

"And money there'll be in it, too, for the captain and those who never let nought but their money sail; but for us there'll be none." It was Keith the foretopman who had spoken. All of the men looked aft at the quarterdeck where the captain, in conversation with Mr. Crane, was walking back and forth.

When watch was changed in the early afternoon, all of the men were called to the main mast. The whole crew gathered there; even the captain's steward slunk out on deck, though he did not stand with the rest of us. The captain, flanked by his two officers, faced us silently, trying to guess our mood before he spoke.

"Men," he began, "the Americans are engaged in a war. We, as Englishmen, must not forget the wounds inflicted upon our nation by this criminal colony of pirates, that turned upon our Monarch and our Flag." The captain paused, as if he expected us to break into cheers.

We stood quietly, waiting for him to continue. Most of us were surprised by the intermission in his speech. For a speech it was, compared to the gruffly spoken orders which were the only words the crew had ever heard the captain address to them before.

"The *Four Winds* is not heading for Boston, but for Charleston. We are carrying guns and powder. Each man on board will receive double pay when we have delivered our cargo." When the captain had finished talking to us, he glared at us, as if his eyes meant to express the contempt which his tongue had left unsaid.

"Any questions?" Captain Mathews asked.

At first no one spoke, but then the voice of old Noah could be heard. "Whoso stoppeth his ears to the cry of the poor, he shall also cry himself, but shall not be hard."

Captain Mathews, who did not know Noah as well as we did, shouted back angrily, "What did you say?"

The carpenter stepped forward and pointed his finger at the captain's red face. "The wicked shall

be cut off from the earth and the transgressors shall
be rooted out of it." Now Noah turned on his heel and
walked away.

The captain followed him with his eyes, as if old
Noah were a ghost; then he turned to Mr. Crane and
mumbled something. Turning on his heel, with the
same determination in his stride as the carpenter's,
the captain walked below.

From his pocket Mr. Crane took a silver case,
opened it and removed a long black cigar. Returning
the case to his pocket, he stared at the cigar. "If any
of you has any questions, I shall be glad to answer
them." Again the cigar was contemplated, then stuck
in the owner's mouth, but still not lighted.

I was not surprised to hear Pimples' voice; indeed,
I think I should have been more surprised if, for once,
he had kept his mouth shut. "Double pay isn't much,"
he grumbled loudly.

Without taking the cigar out of his mouth, Mr.
Crane remarked, "I think it's a lot for a man who isn't
worth his salt beef."

The men laughed. This time, I did not join them,
for I was still watching the mate, who looked upon
us as if he had expected us to laugh, yet despised us
for doing it.

"This run to Charleston is not much more danger-
ous than a run to Boston," he said. At last Mr. Crane
lighted his cigar. When he was puffing on it, having
returned to his pocket the metal box containing
the flint and the twist, he glanced at us quizzically.

The men remained silent, though I think many of them wanted to say exactly what they had jeered at Pimples for saying.

"Get on with your work; we'll sail without lanterns until we reach Charleston."

As soon as the crew had walked forward, their muteness left them; and there was no end of complaining and cursing. I walked to the bow of the ship and climbed out on the bowsprit.

What went round in my head were words — Yankees, civil war, slavery, Boston, Charleston — sounds so meaningless that they might as well have been words in a foreign language; they were like signposts leading to places in a country where I had never been.

"Slavery," I murmured. Well, had I not been a slave in my uncle's house? And how little had I liked it! But the slaves in America were black; maybe they were different from me. I had only seen a Negro once. He had walked past whistling as he went by. He had worn a sailor's outfit. If people didn't like being slaves, why didn't they just revolt? I asked myself.

Ashamed, I shook my head: Why hadn't I rebelled against my uncle? Why had I allowed my aunt to steal my blanket? I knew well, from my own back, that a beating can break your spirit.

My first memories were of love, of my mother's kisses and of her laughter; for she had laughed much and her laughter was like the wind on a summer day. We had been very poor; but my mother had worn her poverty outside and never let it slip into her heart. She had not been bitter; and therefore, she had not needed meekness to hide her hatred behind. Fate had been unkind to her but had not been able to make her unkind. Twelve years of love is a good ballast to sail the seas with, more than enough for many a storm.

The captain was again on the quarterdeck with his telescope. Once more my thoughts returned to war. What did I know about Cromwell and the English Civil War? King Charles had been killed. Cromwell had been called Ironsides. It had all happened so long ago that it belonged almost in the world of fairy tales my mother had told me. Then it occurred to me that one day, a hundred years from now, some children in America would think of this war, which was going on now in their country, just as I did about the revolt against King Charles.

I climbed down from the bowsprit, for I wanted to talk to Rolf.

Rolf was in the cookhouse slicing meat. I sat down upon the coal box and watched him.

"Who is right: the people in the north or the people in the south?"

Rolf put down his knife, folded his arms across his chest, and looked at me. "Jim, my boy, once when I was very young like you, I took a berth on a slaver. We sailed along the coast of Africa and bought men and women, as though they were coconuts. Before we reached Rio de Janeiro, half of them were dead." Rolf picked up his knife again, as though he were go-

ing to continue his work; but instead he turned
quickly and said, "No, Jim, slavery is the greatest
crime there is."

The cook sat down beside me. "When something
horrible happens to you, you remember only a part
of it — sometimes, it isn't even an important part.

"When the slaves died at sea, we threw them to the
sharks, but I can't really remember that . . . I mean,
if I close my eyes, I do not see it. But when we came
to Rio de Janeiro, and those slaves who had survived
the voyage were brought out of the hold . . ." The
cook put his hands across his eyes. "There was a young
girl. Maybe, she was only fourteen or fifteen. She had
a baby in her arms. It was dead. It had been dead for a
long time." Again Rolf made the same motion with
his hand. "One of the seamen took the dead baby and
threw it over the bulwark, into the sea.

"I saw the eyes of that girl, for I was standing
nearby. And, Jim, boy, had they been filled with hatred, I might have forgotten them, but they weren't;
they were like the eyes of a blind person. And I
thought, We've blinded her! And by God, my boy,
we would have been more merciful if we had killed
her."

I tried to think of the girl, and of a blind man's eyes;
but being still a child and wanting an end to all
stories, I said, "What happened to her?"

"She was sold together with the other slaves, I suppose. She was a very pretty girl. I have never sailed
on a slaver since. And no fire in hell can be hot

enough for those who deal in slavery."

"The people of the north are right," I said confidently, pleased with myself for having chosen the right side from the start, for I readily convinced myself that I had been against slavery before talking to Rolf.

"If it is to get rid of slavery they are fighting the south, then they are right."

"But isn't it?"

I sounded so confused and so earnest that Rolf laughed. "Jim, my boy, it matters not to a slave why he is given liberty, just so long as he gets it."

"I am for the north and so are you!" I exclaimed.

Rolf nodded; yet he looked so very sad that I wanted to say something that might change his mood. "Rolf," I asked, "do you know anything about King Charles?"

The cook did not reply. "I mean . . . You know, that war a long time ago in which many people died . . ."

"Yes?"

"Well, you know nobody knows anything about that now, except schoolmasters."

Rolf cocked his head, to show that he was trying to be interested.

"Well, one day it will be like that, about the slave girl and us." Somehow, the thoughts that had been so clear in my mind, when they became words in my mouth, did not seem to make much sense.

"You mean everything will be forgotten?"

Happily, I nodded my head, though this wasn't exactly what I meant.

"When that slave girl is dead, and I am dead, then her suffering is dead, too. It will be as if it hadn't happened at all?"

I nodded again, though this time not so gaily.

Rolf said angrily, "Then it doesn't matter if you free the slaves or not; then nothing matters!"

I walked out of the cookhouse, for I was filled with shame.

How a Squall Settled an Argument

8

THE WEATHER CONTINUED FAIR, with a light breeze blowing from southeast. A sailing ship puts on her best clothes in a storm; for fair weather any old rags will do. The sails of the *Four Winds* were hardly more than rags; and the carpenter, who was also the sailmaker, spent much of his time in patching them. The rigging of a ship needs constant adjustment. The stays that are tightened one day may be slack the next. A new rope may need tightening only a few hours after it has been set up. The man on land sees the ship glide by, with its sails set, and he thinks of a swan, and his heart beats with envy for the men aboard. The ship has sailed past like a vision, and when he returns from his walk and is seated at his dinner, he talks about it as he would of a dream. He did not see the little spot in the rigging, which was a boy with a bucket, tarring the ropes.

I spent much of my time in the rigging with a tar bucket, the sun beating on my back. I was careful not to let the tar drip down on the deck far below, not only because the mate or the captain would curse me, but because the work of removing the spots would be mine.

It is true that on most ships the officers and the crew

fear each other; and therefore, the officers are cruel
and the men sullen. The officers believe that an idle
tar is a mutinous one, and so they keep poor jack
working. Captain Mathews hated us, though I doubt
that he feared us; but this Mr. Goodfellow certainly
did. That was why he would haze us one minute,
and try to make up to the older seamen in a comradely
way, the next. His efforts gained him only the disre-
spect of the crew, for we could distinguish the note of
fear, even in his curses. I felt sorry for him. The job
of second mate is a thankless one. To the captain and
the first mate, he is a whipping boy; and to the men,

a slave driver. Often it is only one voyage since he was a jolly jack in the forecastle, a captain of the foretop, admired by his fellow sailors; and now he is a lonely man on the quarterdeck, eating the captain's leavings.

Mr. Crane did not hate us, for he was too proud to hate anyone who was below him. The first mate walked through the world a self-made king; but kings are lonely, and when they search for friendship, they find flattery; and when they search for love, their quest leads them only to the still pool of a slave's eyes, wherein they find mirrored their own kingliness. The sailors admired Mr. Crane. Although they were frightened of him, and at the outset of the voyage they had all grumbled against him, he was an excellent seaman. He asked much of the men; but nothing that he could not have done — both more quickly and better — himself. I have seen him climb to the top of the mast to let down a royal, before the man behind him had reached the crosstree. The only man aboard who did not care for Mr. Crane was the cook. Rolf disliked the mate; I don't know if he knew why himself. Perhaps it was because he truly loved man, and he felt that Mr. Crane was the chicken hawk, that would empty his roost.

Now that we were so far south, the watch at liberty seldom, during the daylight hours, went below; instead they sat in groups either talking or repairing their clothes. Just as a ship is ever in need of repair, so are jack's clothes; and many a woman might envy the nimbleness with which sailors can steer a needle and thread.

"Any one of you know Jack Hogan?" Keith the fore-topman looked from one to the other of the four men sitting near him.

"Him that is owner of the Sailors' Rest?" asked Squinty.

"Yes, my boy. That same one-legged pirate, who will pilot any sailor across an ocean of beer to wreck him on the stony beach of poverty. Yes, that is the man."

"I ain't ever been introduced to him personally. But I have drunk a pint of half-and-half in his establishment; and me thinks it was half bilge water and half pure poison with a little soap mixed in it for flavor."

Blackie laughed, which made Squinty turn around and glare at him, as though he thought the younger sailor had meant to insult him.

"That is him, my lad," Keith said to Squinty, who was old enough to be his father. "But as for the soap, it must have gotten in accidentally, for old Jack Hogan wouldn't spoil his customers with favors like that." Keith was patching a torn jacket; and for the moment, the work at hand was so difficult that he could not sew and speak at the same time.

"Slaving," he began again, "that is how Jack Hogan got his money . . . And that is how he lost his leg."

Pimples, who was sitting next to Blackie clumsily

darning a pair of socks with a needle that would have been of better use to a young lady doing cross-stitch, said, "His leg was eaten by cannibals, it was."

Keith acted as if he had not heard Pimples, but Blackie who was a great admirer of Keith the foretopman looked down at Pimples' socks and remarked, "That is right pretty work, M'am, for a fancy pillow."

Pimples spat on the deck. Lately, Shanghai had been paying a little attention to Pimples, which made him more arrogant towards the rest of us. Pimples would have liked to have been a comrade of Keith's, and had Keith blown the whistle, Pimples would have jumped right smartly to attention; but the foretopman had no use for him.

"Ever heard of the ship *The Southern Cross*, Blackie?" Keith asked.

"There was a small lugger by that name; but I don't know if that's the one you mean."

"This ship was a hermaphrodite brig, and as pretty a little ship as you could think of. I saw her myself when I was but a child. Then she was sailing in the Irish trade, and they had schooner-rigged her. A crime it was, and she died from the shame of it. She was wrecked on the Isle of Man. But the time I am talking about is long ago, when she was rigged as a hermaphrodite, as I told you.

"My father has told me this story, himself, and he was a gospel-fearing man, that never told anything but the truth, if he could help it. *The Southern Cross* was bound for the slave trade. Her master was part owner. He was a redheaded man that was no better than the whiskey that he drank. The first mate was a Dane or a Swede; but he doesn't figure because he fell overboard before they had kissed Land's End. The second mate, who had never sailed as mate before, got promoted to the first mate's berth; so they had to find another second mate. The crew said they wanted the carpenter, whose name was Jack Hogan. The captain didn't care; he just doubled Jack's wages and told him to move aft. Now the first mate was a good sailor, but he wasn't much of an officer. He was scared of the crew and cursing them all the time." Here Keith paused for a moment and looked aft, where Mr. Goodfellow was pacing the quarterdeck.

"Now Jack Hogan," Keith continued, "wasn't afraid of anybody. He would have sailed *The Southern Cross* with the devil's grandmother as bosun, and her grandson as crew. The captain liked to exercise with his bottles in the privacy of his cabin; and soon Jack was more master of *The Southern Cross* than he was.

"They picked up their cargo in some port in Africa and were to deliver it in Jamaica. That was when the slave trade was still respectable for a Christian gentleman. Well, on their way to Jamaica, fully loaded, they were becalmed for more than a fortnight. By the end of that time, they had lost half of their cargo; and the only ones that were happy were the sharks. Some of the crew had gone overboard, too; and so had the first mate. He had got sick with a fever — at least, that's what Jack Hogan said when he got to Jamaica.

"One night the slaves got loose, and there was the devil to pay. They murdered the captain and all the crew. Only Jack survived. He climbed to the foretop with four loaded pistols; and every time a slave tried to climb up to get him, he shot him down. Well, the slaves couldn't sail the ship, so they made a bargain with Jack that if he would sail them back to Africa, they wouldn't kill him. Jack went along on the bargain, but he did not sail *The Southern Cross* to Africa, but straight to Jamaica; and when those poor slaves saw the harbor and one of His Majesty's frigates that was anchored there, they went for Jack, and he had to climb the mast again with his pistols. But this time one of those poor unfortunates got Jack in the leg with a knife. But Jack made out all right though; for he had saved the ship and some of the cargo; and the owners in Bristol paid him enough so that he could go back and buy the Sailors' Rest. But he lost his leg. That wound the Negro had made wasn't even deep, but it festered and wouldn't heal, so they cut his leg off. It was out in the Bay of Jamaica, they did it; and they threw the leg to the sharks. The next day, there were six of them murdering fishes lying with bellies all pretty and white on the surface of the water. But sharks are clever. They figured something was wrong and never ate any of those six dead sharks, which was too bad, for if they had, there wouldn't be a shark alive in the oceans today. They would have been poi-

soned, all of them, by Jack Hogan's leg. A regular bad
one, he is.

"Some say it was himself that loosened those slaves,
and that he, and not a slave, cut the captain's throat,
to send him on his last journey. But that is all hear-
say, and I wouldn't repeat it, for there's no point in
telling lies about a man like Jack Hogan, when the
truth is bad enough."

Keith put his thread between his teeth and bit it
over, for his work was finished; then he held out his
jacket to admire it. "As I said, Jack Hogan was a regular bad one, and he ain't grown better with years, as
whiskey does. And I'll tell you something else,
which'll come as a surprise to you all." Keith paused
and looked about the group that was listening so at-
tentively to his story; by now it numbered all of starboard watch and even a couple of men from larboard.
"I will tell you that part owner of this old tub is Jack
Hogan of the Sailors' Rest, late gentleman slaver and
one of the worst rascals in all of England."

We all looked up with amazement at Keith. Shanghai, who was one of them from larboard who had
stopped his work to listen to Keith, said, "Black men
ain't got no souls. It is no more wrong to sell them
than to sell a dog."

"I would rather sail with a black man as companion than I would with you!" Keith retorted.

"This ain't a ship but a floating chapel. This ain't
a group of jolly tars but a prayer meeting of old la-
dies."

Keith jumped up and everyone stepped back to give the men room to fight.

But there was to be no fight that day. Just as Keith and Shanghai were about to close in on each other, we heard Mr. Goodfellow calling, "Ahoy all men to save sail! Furl the royals and the topsails. Come on, my hearties!"

Stunned with surprise, for there was hardly a wind moving, we looked out over the sea. To the southeast, a great cloud bank was moving rapidly towards us.

We had just furled the royals, when the squall hit us. Hanging on for our lives in the yards, while trying to furl the topsails, we saw the *Four Winds* below us; she was racing through the sea in a cascade of white foam.

Keith the foretopman was near me. I looked at him and smiled, to tell him of my sympathy. He winked and put up his thumb.

By the time we had the *Four Winds* all tight — if not Bristol fashion — it was our watch. As the men of larboard went below, I saw Shanghai talking eagerly to one of the boys on his watch; the one the men called Fatty.

A Ship Divided

9

As THE *Four Winds*, with a wind too fair for its foul cargo drew near the coast of America, that war which had been declared between its northern and southern states divided the crew of our ship. Keith the foretopman was the natural leader of what we called the Yankees, and Shanghai, the noisy leader of the slavers. I do not think that those who were for slavery knew why they supported it. Pimples and Fatty had by life been so robbed that only the color of their skin and their nationality were left. Pimples, naturally, was the loudest of the two. He felt that the existence of Negro slaves made him into a gentleman; and that the castle, which was rightfully his, was just beyond the horizon.

Fatty, not being able to use his tongue — language was a tool with which he could not form sentences much longer than the most common curses — took the opportunity of showing his newly discovered knighthood by tying a tar bucket on the tail of poor Potiphar.

Before one starts mistreating those who are weaker than one's self, it is wise to find out whether they have any friends to avenge them. Potiphar, being a cat who could only explain his misery by a loud *meow*, would seem a safe enough victim to torture for a young gentleman, who for the moment was short of slaves to amuse himself with. Unfortunately for poor Fatty, Potiphar had many friends among the crew. Two of them, Rolf the cook and Noah the carpenter, brought quick relief to the cat by untying the string which held fast the tar bucket; and within minutes they had punished Potiphar's enemy, as well. While Rolf held the culprit, the carpenter, with the end of a rope, made that part of the body which is handy when you want to sit down unusable for poor Fatty for several hours.

Now I should like to be able to say that we, the Yankees, were a fine group of men, whose lack of wings and haloes was merely due to an oversight of God. But this would be as untrue as the claim that all the slavers had horns and a tail like Potiphar's for us to tie our hate upon. Many of the Yankees had chosen not to be slavers because they hated Captain Mathews and loved our own leader, Keith. Most had never seen a Negro, or, as I, had seen only one by chance in the streets of Bristol or Liverpool, but had never exchanged a word with other than white men.

Keith believed in his own freedom; and being a generous tar, he wanted to share it with others. His concept of freedom did not need the frame of others' slavery.

Will Hanley, an old tar, chose our side because we were the most numerous and the strongest group; and he believed that right was always with the majority. This meant that so long as Will was in the forecastle, he supported us; but the moment he heard the bosun blow his whistle or the voice of Captain Mathews, all thoughts of rebellion disappeared from his mind. His sort is not uncommon; and as pieces of wood without keel or rudder, their course through life is determined by the currents and the winds.

"A man is set on earth to do his duty and to obey those whom God in His wisdom has placed above him," the bosun said to the carpenter. It was nearly noon and both watches were on deck.

"It is written that Moses spoke unto Pharaoh and Pharaoh listened."

The bosun shook his head. "We are tars, not prophets; and you do your white beard no honor by sowing the seeds of mutiny among the men."

"Mutiny." Old Noah mumbled the word as though its meaning was unknown to him. "I speak not my own words, for they are like the chaff is to the wheat. I speak the words of the Lord."

Shanghai, who stood near the bosun, laughed; and the bosun's face grew red. "You make the words of the Lord your own. Captain Mathews ain't Pharaoh, though me thinks there are an abundance of plagues aboard this ship." The bosun's final sentence had been addressed to Shanghai, not to the carpenter.

Without anyone having noticed him, Mr. Goodfellow approached the group. He yelled at Shanghai, "What are you standing there gaping for? Have you no work? If not, I'll find some for you!"

Shanghai touched his sailor's hat and walked
away. The bosun followed his example. Those of us
who were at liberty quickly retreated to the fore part
of the ship. Only the carpenter remained motionless,
deep in thought. Mr. Goodfellow stared at the old
man, who stood as still as Lot's wife; then the mate
shrugged his shoulders and walked aft. As soon as
the officer had returned to the quarterdeck, old Noah
turned and walked forward, passing us as though he
had not seen us.

The bosun had sent three of the crew up the rigging to tighten a rope and was directing their work
from the deck. The bosun was a perfect petty officer,
liked by the officers and respected by the men. By
right of skill he should have been a captain; but the
bosun, in spite of his strength and abilities, could only
repeat an order, not give one, himself. Having only
his eyes to see with, the horizon was the limit of his
world. He was a man who was loyal to his master. He
had not the imagination to envision a world different
from the one he lived in. The *Four Winds* was carrying weapons and ammunition for the Confederacy;
Captain Mathews was its master, and he the bosun. To
Charleston he would sail the ship, for doing his duty
was the bosun's religion. As he would have said himself, it is not for the likes of him to question. Indeed,
he would have thought such an act to be a kind of
treason. Many a slaver has sailed with such men
among the crew; and many a jack tar has been cruelly
flogged for nought but having aroused the captain's

disfavor, with such a man as the bosun handling the whip.

The bosun had spoken of mutiny; and it was true that many of the men had whispered as much, while Keith the foretopman had spoken of it aloud.

"But from the word to the act is many days sailing," Rolf explained that evening when I was sitting in the cookhouse.

"We could lock the captain and Mr. Crane up in their cabins. As for Mr. Goodfellow, he — "

Rolf, who had smiled while listening to me, interrupted, "And Shanghai, Pimples, and half of larboard watch — where are you going to lock them up? In the forecastle? And what about the bosun? There'll be a lot of bloodshed when you take over the *Four Winds*."

In my mind's eye, I saw the bosun, who had never been unkind to me, being murdered, and I grimaced as if I were in pain.

"Jim, my boy, life is not roast beef; it is a stew and there are many things in it which are hard to swallow."

"But it isn't right," I mumbled.

Rolf took out his pipe and his tobacco pouch. "Jim, slavery has long since been forbidden most places; and it will die before long of its own accord in America, too. It won't make much difference whether they get the powder and guns aboard the *Four Winds* or not."

I remembered Rolf's anger when I had explained

to him my thought that all suffering becomes history. "The powder and the guns will kill someone."

The cook lighted his pipe. "Jim, my boy, when you and I are in Charleston, we'll run away. We'll go north and fight with the Yankees."

I nodded, for I had had similar thoughts myself; yet I was not satisfied. I had felt the same way as a child, when having been naughty and made my mother unhappy, I had resolved to repent by making some silly vow, such as not eating any of the cherries from our tree when spring came. I looked up at Rolf. I wanted to insist that it would be more help to the

northern states if the *Four Winds* never reached Charleston; instead I stood up and and walked to the door of the cookhouse.

"Jim . . ."

I turned and Rolf smiled sadly; I knew from the expression in his eyes that our thoughts were the same.

The sun had set, but it was still light. The horizon was blood-red and the sea purple. As I made my way forward, I saw Pimples. I wanted to avoid speaking with him, but he called to me. He was sitting down, leaning against the bowsprit.

"Jim, when we get to Charleston, I am going to join that little war."

I said nothing. There was no point in asking which side he would be on. Telling him that I hoped he would be shot in the first battle in which he fought would only have gotten me into a fight. Pimples was four years older and a head taller than I.

"When the war is over, they are going to give two slaves to every man that fought and four to every officer."

"How do you know that?"

Pimples laughed as though I had told him a joke. "Shanghai told me." I could not help asking when Shanghai had last been in America, and how he had learned this news. Pimples replied proudly, "I will fight, even if I get no slaves. I'll do it because it's right."

Near the foremast, Keith and Blackie were sitting and talking. They didn't hear my approach.

"The captain and Mr. Crane, we could lock up in their cabins," Keith said. Blackie nodded enthusiastically.

I turned from them and walked to the rigging. I climbed to the crosstree and looked out over the sea: the endless sea. No, it was not endless. There in the west, where the sun had set, was land. All of a sudden I heard the screech of a bird. I looked up. Two gulls were flying above me, circling the ship. "American gulls," I whispered. They looked no different from the gulls that flew over Bristol; but in mid-ocean there are no birds. Tomorrow or the next day, someone would call out, "Land ahoy!"

Land Ahoy!

10

IT WAS THE MORNING WATCH, two days after I had seen
the first birds. The sky was cloudless and the breeze
came from the southeast. I was sitting on the crosstree, having been ordered up there as lookout. The
ship moved lazily in the swells; below the starboard
watch was busily swabbing the deck. Not long before, I had seen a school of dolphins. How I envied
their power and their freedom! Few animals are so
graceful as that little whale. When it leaps out of the
sea, it appears so much part of the water that I have
often wondered if God created the sea so that he
could have the pleasure of creating the dolphin.

"Ahoy up there! Can you see anything?" It was Mr.
Crane's voice. I looked towards the west. On the hori-
zon there seemed to be a low bank of clouds or a haze.
It was bluish in color: Could it be land?

"There are clouds, sir, or a haze in the west."

Mr. Crane was gazing up at me. Though I could
not distinguish his features, I was sure he wore an expression of disgust. He took hold of the rigging and
within seconds he was beside me. "It is land, boy."
Mr. Crane was shielding his eyes from the bright
glare of the sun's rays on the sea.

"It is land," he repeated.

"I'm sorry, sir. I . . ."

"The land is very low; what we are seeing are the clouds just above it."

"Is it Charleston, sir?" I asked timidly.

Mr. Crane laughed. "We are south of it, but no more than two days sailing, if the wind keeps." The mate must have been able to see in my face how unwelcome this news was to me. "Wars are always fought by fools," he said. "The fool is the horse that the clever man rides."

I turned away from Mr. Crane, not because his face was evil, but because it was handsome and intelligent. "But slavery, sir!"

Mr. Crane, who with his left hand was holding onto a shroud, made a sweep of the ship with his right arm. "And what do you think these are, free men? There exist only slaves and masters, choose your side, Jim." Then in a low voice, as though he was speaking to himself rather than to me, he added, "God knows if it will make you happier to be a master."

Mr. Crane was already climbing down. I watched him and thought, He is better at navigating than the captain and better at climbing than Keith, yet he must be wrong.

Again I looked out to the west, and the bank of clouds seemed to be changing color. "Thieves and Indians" — my uncle's words came back to me, and I laughed at them. I marveled at how much I had changed since I had stood in my uncle's office, only a few weeks before, and seen Captain Mathews for the first time. I am still a boy, I thought, but anyway, I am a sailor. And it is good to be a sailor. Good to sit in the crosstree of a ship and feel the wind blowing through your hair.

From far below, I could hear the carpenter strike the bell; my watch was finished. Still I had to remain in the rigging until someone came up to relieve me. Shading my eyes, I looked searchingly in all directions.

"Ahoy!" Jack's smiling face was just below the crosstree. "Where is land?"

"There," I said and pointed west.

"Not much to look at," he replied and shielded his eyes as Mr. Crane had done.

"It is flat," I explained a little smugly. "What we are looking at are clouds just above it. We are two days south of Charleston."

Sitting down beside me, Jack whispered in my ear, "That's good, for our plan isn't finished . . . There are too many we can't trust. Keith thinks we should take over the boat and sail her to New York. We would get a big reward for it."

I remembered Pimples' statement, "Every man who fights in the war will get two slaves."

Perhaps Jack guessed my thoughts, for unexpectedly he confided, "Not that I care, but the old folks are poor. My father can't work; he fell from the rigging and spoiled his back. Something's broken the doctors say."

Jack had never spoken of his family before. "My

father was a sailor, too," I said, "but he was lost at sea."

"That's too bad, Jim," he remarked sadly. For several moments we both were silent, as this was the only way we knew of paying respect to the dead; then Jack continued, "My father was a bosun in the China trade, been fifteen times round the Cape of Good Hope." No less proudly he added, "My mother didn't want me to go to sea; she cries properly every time I leave."

Suddenly I found myself envying Jack, envying him his parents and his dream of returning home to Bristol with a reward; and I was ashamed that I had been suspicious of his motives for wanting to sail the *Four Winds* to New York.

"How old are you?" I asked.

"Fourteen," he answered, and too late I realized that he would now ask me the same question. "How old are you?"

I thought of lying, of saying fourteen, or at least thirteen, as my uncle had claimed I was to Captain Mathews. "Twelve," I replied softly. It was the evil thought I had had about Jack, when he spoke about the reward, that made me tell the truth. Hastily, I added, "My uncle told the captain that I was thirteen."

Jack looked at me with surprise. "You are small; but I thought you were fourteen."

I felt so pleased that Jack had thought me older than I was, that I laughed. Jack laughed, too. I saw a school of dolphins ahead of the ship and pointed to them. It was a large school, twenty at least. When they reached the bow of the ship, they turned and followed us. They leapt above the waves as if they were too happy to be satisfied with only the waters of the sea, but needed to play in the sky as well.

When I was down on deck again, I walked to the forecastle and climbed down into the twilight of our cabin. Nobody was there. The weather was too fair for anyone to spend his time in the foul air below. I didn't know why I myself had gone below. I sat down at the bench beside the table. A dim light came from the small skylight above me. Here I had lived for almost a month, and the smell of the rotten water in the bilge no longer seemed strange or unpleasant: it was the smell of home.

Beyond the wall that the table stood up against was the forward hold. On the starboard side there was a small door which led into the hold. It surprised me that the door was not locked, but only closed by two ordinary hasps. I undid the hasps; and to my amazement, when I pulled on it only lightly, the door opened. Doors like this one, I thought, you should only be able to open by exerting enormous strength or by saying a magic word.

The air streaming out of the open door felt cool and not unpleasant. A ladder led from the door to the bottom of the hold. I had not really planned to enter that dark cavern, but a noise from above told me that someone was coming into the forecastle; and without thinking, I stepped onto the top rung of the ladder and closed the door. The door stayed closed, even though the hasps were not fastened.

Slowly I climbed down the ladder, counting each step. There were ten. Once in the hold, I stood completely still, listening to the noises of the ship. It groaned like a sick animal, while the waves tapped at the hull with ghostly fingers. I held my hands out in front of me; they touched the rough wood of some boxes. What was in them: guns or ammunition? I fumbled from the starboard to the larboard side of the ship, where there was room enough for me to walk aft. I hesitated. I was frightened and wanted to return to the deck and the sight of the sky; yet I walked on.

The ship had two holds. I came to the wooden wall that divided them, and followed it. Soon I reached a ladder like the one which had led me from the forecastle. I climbed it and came to a small door. To my surprise, it was standing open. From a crack between two boards in the covering of the aft hatch, a dim light spread over the hold. As the other hold, this one was filled with wooden boxes of different sizes and a large number of barrels, which I supposed contained powder.

Suddenly I heard a noise from the bottom of the aft hold, almost directly below me. Quickly I climbed down the ladder; someone was climbing the ladder on the opposite side of the wall. In my confusion, I turned right, and ran along the wall. When I came midway, the passage was blocked. I stood still. I could hear the man grunt as he pushed his way through the low door.

I was trapped. I sat down on the planks, trying to make myself as small as possible. The man who had entered the hold was an older man. I was sure of that, for he breathed heavily and moved clumsily. The man was standing still.

"Anyone here?" he called, and I recognized the voice at once. It was Captain Mathews. I didn't answer, assuming that if he had seen me, he would have called out my name.

I was sitting on the deck of the hold, both my palms outstretched, resting on the rough planks. All of a sudden I felt something gently touching one of my hands. I pulled it away and heard a rat scurrying down the corridor towards the captain.

It must have run through the captain's legs, for I heard him curse and mumble, "This is one cargo I won't share with you." But the sight of the rat must have dismissed his suspicion that he was not in the hold alone. He climbed the ladder again, and closed the door behind him. I tried to stand up; but my legs were shaking, and I had to lean against one of the boxes for fear I should fall.

Now I had only one thought: to return to the forecastle, and from there to the deck and the sweet sight of the sun. Still I waited a while for fear that the captain might hear me. "One . . . two . . . three . . ." I counted slowly until I reached a hundred; only then did I dare to move.

When I came to the wall of the forepart of the hold, I thought with fear that someone might have entered the forecastle, and seeing the hasps undone, might have fastened them; and I would be locked in this dark and dismal hold. At that moment the door opened, and what seemed to me a very bright light flooded the hold. It was the flame of the candle which the carpenter held in his hand as he climbed down the ladder. I flattened myself against the wall, as I thought desperately, Doesn't he know that this place is filled with powder?

The light of the candle blinded me. Old Noah had seen me. He crooked his finger and slowly I walked towards him. A space away from him I stopped. In the light of the candle old Noah's beard looked doubly white, and his face, tanned by the sun and wind, almost brown.

"What are you doing here, boy?"

I could not answer, for what was there to say? Could I say that I had merely come down in the hold, because being alone in the forecastle I had noticed the small door? "The captain was here," I whispered. "Now he has returned to the aft hold." I looked down at my feet.

"Did he see you, that Beelzebub?"

I shook my head; and for some reason which I do not know, I noticed that the planks under my feet were old and worn. The carpenter was contemplating the cargo; and watching him, I was reminded of a picture I had once seen at Sunday School of Moses.

"Those who live by the sword, shall die by it."
Noah was not talking to me; and the thought struck
me that maybe he only talked to God. "With fire did
the Lord destroy Sodom, and only the righteous es-
caped."

The sight of the candle's flickering flame and the
thought of the powder that surrounded us made me
cry out, "The candle, sir!"

The carpenter looked at the candle as if he had
not seen it before. His hand rose so that the flame was
in front of his eyes. "When Thou lightest the lamps,
the seven lamps shall give light over and against the
candlestick."

I knew that Noah's words were from the Bible, that
book from which my mother had read to me so often,
yet I could not recall ever having heard such strange
things as old Noah knew by heart.

"The Lord rained upon Sodom and Gomorrah
brimstone and fire from the Lord out of heaven."

Without knowing why, I said aloud, "No."

The carpenter turned towards me. "The words of
the Lord are holy and you may not speak against
them."

I remembered what the bosun had said about old
Noah using the words of God to suit his own pur-
poses, but I said nothing, for at that moment I knew
that the man facing me was mad. The mad live in a
world populated with shadows, and the voices of the
living cannot reach them.

"If thou goest against the word of the Lord, the Lord will slay thee."

I nodded my head vigorously, for I was certain that if I raised my voice against the old man, surely he would kill me.

Without warning, the carpenter smiled and even laughed. "You are a good child."

"Thank you," I whispered.

"The captain is a wicked man."

"Yes," I agreed loudly, for I was saying something that I believed.

"The tool of the Lord is often a humble man, for he scorned kings and his only son was a carpenter. Come let us go back to the face of God and the sun."

I turned quickly and made my way to the ladder. When I reached the door, the carpenter whispered, "Wait, listen first, then look and see if anyone is in the forecastle."

I heard nothing. Slowly I opened the door. The cabin was empty. I climbed into the forecastle. The carpenter followed me, and closed the door behind us. "Speak not of this."

"No, sir," I whispered and then ran to the ladder, and climbed up to the deck.

I ran in search of Rolf. I found him talking to Keith the foretopman. The cook noticed me at once. "What's the matter, boy? You are shaking. You look as if you'd seen a ghost."

Then I realized that I had nothing to say! What

was there to tell? I looked back towards the forecastle. The carpenter was standing in the entrance
watching me. "No, where should I have seen a ghost?
I fell asleep and had a bad dream."

I walked over to the railing and looked out over
the sea. There were no dolphins to be seen. What
should I have said to Rolf: that the carpenter was mad
and would blow us all to kingdom come? No . . .
No, I could not have said that without it being told
to Mr. Crane, who would in turn tell it to Captain
Mathews, and he would have the old man flogged
and put in irons.

Jack was still sitting in the crosstree. How much
time had gone by since I was sitting there beside him
and we had laughed together? Then I recalled that
I had thought of myself as a sailor and it had made
me happy. "No, I am a child," I whispered to the sea.
Looking down into the foam along the side of the
ship, I saw a single dolphin swimming. It is an omen,
I thought, a good omen. I felt the sun warm on my
back; then I heard Rolf's and Keith's laughter.

"Little dolphin, bring me luck," I whispered. The
dolphin dived deep down and then shot up through
the water and into the air, its curved back glistening
in the sun.

A Fight

11

THE NIGHT AFTER MY MEETING with old Noah in the hold of the ship, I slept badly. Strange and horrible dreams came to me; I would awaken, listen to the breathing of sleeping men, then I, too, would fall asleep, only to be awakened by a nightmare a short time later. Finally, I decided to get up and go out on deck. Before I left the forecastle, I tiptoed over to the carpenter's bunk. He was sleeping so peacefully that for a moment I almost believed that my meeting with him had been part of a nightmare, my most terror-filled dream. But I glanced towards the center of the cabin; even in the dim light of the single small oil lamp, I could see the fastened hasps on the small door.

It was a beautiful night. The sky was cloudless and the stars shone so brightly that I almost wished that day would not come. I smiled to myself, remembering how I once had walked with my uncle at night in Bristol. He had taken me along because he had purchased a sack of potatoes cheaply and wanted me to carry it home. He had remarked upon the brightness of the stars by saying, "They look like newly minted shillings." Everything pleasant to my uncle was connected with money; these stars would have reminded him of half-crown pieces.

I climbed over the railing and out upon the bowsprit. Sitting across it with a leg dangling on either side, I looked down into the water. The foam at the bow of the ship was luminous. This was the first time that I saw the fire of the sea; since, I have been told that it is caused by millions of small animals, which are so tiny that the human eye cannot see them individually. How strange and beautiful nature is; the mother of all things, who cares more for beauty than she does for justice, goodness, or any of the other phantoms that man, the half-god, invents and uses injustice and cruelty to defend.

Dawn was beginning to break. The stars paled and the sky in the east was streaked with white and gray. I climbed back onto the deck and looked up to see who was on lookout in the crosstree. It was Shanghai; he had been watching me. This was the slavers' watch, though far from everyone on larboard watch was a slaver. Mr. Goodfellow was walking back and forth on the quarterdeck; often he stopped to look up at the masts. Some of larboard watch were sitting around the foremast talking. I walked over to join them; but then I saw that Fatty was among them, and I changed my mind. Since Rolf and the carpenter had thrashed Fatty for the trick he had played on Potiphar, Fatty had been very surly to me.

Now the horizon in the east was growing red. The

sun would soon be up. How different the sunrises and sunsets were here from those in Bristol, where the sun gets up slowly like an old man, and stays at eve as though it were a friend who hated to say good-bye. The stars were gone. In the west I could make out the low land which was America.

"When we get to Charleston, I will get even with you, all of you!"

I had not heard Fatty's approach, so I was startled by his voice. "I haven't done anything," I said quickly.

"You!" Fatty shouted and sputtered. "You don't even know my name!"

I was embarrassed; Fatty was right; I did not know his name, and had always called him by his nickname.

"You are only a boy!" Fatty's cheeks were flushed with anger and his hands were knotted into fists. Fatty was fourteen; and he accepted that grownups by right of age and strength could call him anything they chose, but not a child like myself.

"What is your name?" I asked apprehensively.

"Gordon, Mickey Gordon."

"I'm sorry, Michael," I said and held out my hand.

"No, you just keep on calling me Fatty, and Mickey Gordon shall fix you. I will go and tell them in Charleston that you are Yankees, and they will hang you." Fatty paused for a moment as though he was out of breath; then he added, "All of you!"

"I won't call you Fatty anymore . . . I promise."

Mickey grinned and looked up at the crosstree, then he hit out at me. I stepped aside and his fist grazed my shoulder.

"A fight! A fight!" some of the younger men on larboard watch cried out.

Mickey attacked me again, but he hit out too wildly; I ducked and his blows did not touch me.

"Young men!" It was Mr. Goodfellow, and Fatty's arms at once fell to his sides, for he feared the officers. "I have no objection to two gentlemen settling an argument by a little fisticuffs. Come along, you two, up on the hatch there." Mr. Goodfellow indicated by a wave of his hand that he meant for us to climb up on the canvas-covered rear hatch.

Most of larboard watch gathered around the hatch. Mr. Goodfellow stood with his hands folded over his chest. "No kicking," he said.

Mickey looked down at his feet and shuffled them on the canvas.

"Come on, Fatty, give the cook's little lamb a licking!" It was Shanghai calling out from the crosstree.

Mickey bit his lip and then came towards me, swinging his fists. "It ain't no boy; it's a windmill," one of the men cried out.

I bent forward and Mickey's blows fell on my back. "Come on, hit him back!" Mr. Goodfellow ordered.

"I'll put sixpence on Jim," the bosun shouted; and Mr. Goodfellow took the bet.

I had backed away to the corner of the hatch.

Mickey was making a strange kind of dance in front
of me, as he prepared to attack me again. You have
got to hit him, I said to myself silently; but again I
stepped aside when his arms swung out at me. His
blow missed me; but because he had put all his
strength into it, he stumbled and fell off the hatch.

Several of the men burst out laughing and I —
though I did not think it funny at all — laughed too.

"Get back up there, and finish him!" Shanghai
shouted.

When he jumped back up on the hatch, Mickey
was trembling with rage. I stepped backwards and
holding up my arms to protect me, tried to avert his
blows. The stinging pain when Fatty hit me near the
ear finally made me hit back. My blow was not hard
and only struck Mickey's shoulder; but it made the
bosun cry out, "Good boy, Jim!"

Now I realized that I would have to take a beating
from Mickey or give him one. When he next came
at me, with his hands flaying the air in front of him,
I aimed a blow at his chest. My fist hit the left side
of his neck, instead. Mickey gasped; the tears
streamed from his eyes.

I wanted to cry out that I was sorry that I had hurt
him, but the voices of the men drove Mickey on. A
moment later, he was attacking me once more. Again
and again Mickey hit my shoulders; then I hit his
chin with my right fist. I had put all my weight behind the blow and Mickey tumbled down upon the
canvas.

"You owe me a sixpence, sir!" the bosun said jubilantly.

Mickey was sitting on the hatch, looking up at me with an expression of both hatred and fear.

"What is going on here?" It was Mr. Crane. I jumped down off the hatch.

Mr. Goodfellow explained to the first mate that we were merely having a gentleman's game of fisticuffs. Mr. Crane looked with disgust at all of us, especially at Mr. Goodfellow, whose face had grown red as he had tried to explain what had happened.

"There are no gentlemen aboard this ship, and I will have no fights. Get back to your work, at once!"

Most of the sailors had already returned to their duties, now the rest of them quickly dispersed; Mr. Crane turned and walked aft.

"You are not on my watch, boy. Get back to your bunk!" Mr. Goodfellow barked at me.

I walked slowly aft, my shoulders and back aching from the beating they had been given.

As I lay staring into the dark room, I thought of Mickey. "He hated me from the start," I almost said aloud.

But my conscience answered, "He hates everyone. He was brought up in the poorhouse, while you — "

"So does Shanghai hate everyone; should I care about him, too?" I interrupted my conscience angrily.

But one's conscience when one is wrong is seldom

tongue-tied; and it quickly replied, "Shanghai is a man, but Fatty is a boy like yourself."

I closed my eyes and tried desperately to think of my mother, and of events that had happened before she died.

A Fire! A Fire!

12

"Starboard watch on deck!"

The voice woke me from sleep. Having lain down fully clothed, I was the first man on deck. The sun was high over the horizon, the breeze was light, and every rag that could be fastened to the rigging was set. Walking midship I saw Mickey Gordon; it occurred to me to try and talk with him; but at my slight smile, he scowled and I turned away. I remembered a saying of my aunt's about it being far more difficult to undo the knots of fate than to tie them.

I was set to cleaning the brass, which gives one time to think, for the work itself requires only the attention of the hands not of the head.

Old Noah, I thought, and turned to look at the carpenter who was standing at the helm. The old man's eyes appeared half-closed. His brown, knotty, weather-beaten hands were resting on the wheel. If I only knew what was in his mind! I thought; then I shuddered, fearing that I did know, for I saw in front of me the kegs of powder in the light of a candle. He thinks he is chosen by God; God who destroyed Sodom and Gomorrah.

Captain Mathews was walking back and forth by

the mainmast. I knew that I could not go to him. Although the carpenter might think he was the prophet of God, the Captain was all-powerful aboard the *Four Winds,* and he was not a forgiving or a merciful man.

Though every minute of every hour, in every day, is exactly the same length, a watch can sometimes seem so long that one would swear that this was not true. As the sun rose higher in the sky, its rays burned my back, and the deck felt so warm beneath my bare feet that I could not stand still.

"Mr. Pond . . ." I jumped as I recognized Captain Mathews' voice behind me.

"Yes, sir," I mumbled and stiffly turned to face him.

"Mr. Pond . . ." he repeated; and then he paused, as if he had forgotten what he wanted to say. "Your guardian asked me to be in a father's place for you."

I nodded and touched my sailor's hat, though I doubted if my uncle could ever have requested such a thing.

"When we come to Charleston, you stay on board."

Again I nodded; then, thinking that not enough, I added, "Yes, sir."

The captain looked searchingly at me, as though he was trying to guess my thoughts. "I shall give you a whipping, if you try to run away."

Again I bobbed my head; but in my thoughts I said "If you catch me . . ." And such is the force of habit and respect for authority that I silently added "sir" to my mute reply.

"Boy or man I shall have them flogged if they don't do their duty."

I looked away from the captain's face, for I could not bear the smile that disfigured his features, as he spoke. He is a devil, I thought.

"Remember it, boy. Nobody disobeys Captain Mathews without regretting it."

I looked up at the captain again; he was frowning now. "Yes, sir," I said loudly.

The captain was looking beyond me at the carpenter who was standing at the wheel. Speaking loud enough for Noah to hear him, he said, "Anyone who mutinies aboard the *Four Winds* will be hanged from the top yard."

At the mentioning of the top yard, I glanced up in the rigging; there I could see Keith and Blackie. The captain also looked aloft; then he said, as though he were talking of something pleasant, "The dance a tar dances with the wind, when he is strung from the rigging, is a pretty dance, but it is his last."

Again the captain was smiling. I turned away from him and started polishing once more. For a while, the captain watched me; then he walked away.

The sun was setting and the land in the west was not blue but red, as if it were on fire. We had eaten. Starboard watch was off-duty, and a group of us were sitting in the bow of the ship enjoying the coolness of the evening air. Keith started to sing, and though his voice was not as beautiful as Rolf's, it had a melancholy tone that was pleasing.

> *The flowers are blooming on the moor,*
> *High ho for my love and me.*
> *The clouds blow east, the clouds blow west,*
> *High ho for my love and me.*
> *The world was made for a tar and his lass,*
> *High ho for my love and me.*
> *In gibbets and prisons men do rot,*

High ho for my love and me.
Kings and queens in castles live,
High ho for my love and me.
I envy not their high abode,
High ho for my love and me.
For I live in my lassie's heart,
High ho for my love and me.
High ho, high ho,
High ho for my love and me.

No one spoke as the voice of Keith died away. We were all watching the setting sun, and some perhaps were thinking of their homes. Next to joy, I believe that melancholy is the pleasantest of all emotions, and I swear that it is not related to sadness at all.

"The world is on fire." Keith's hand rose as he spoke, and he pointed towards land.

"Aye, it is," Squinty said. "I can even smell smoke."

"I can, too," said Will Hanley; and we all began to sniff at the air.

With horror we realized that our imagination was not playing tricks on us. There was a fire aboard the *Four Winds!*

"It comes from the forecastle!" Keith shouted; and many of the men started in that direction in order to try to save their belongings, which, though paltry, were all that many of them possessed.

I looked around the deck for the carpenter; but he was not to be seen. "The fire's in the hold!" I cried.

"We'll all be blown to kingdom come!" cried one

of the older sailors in such a strange voice that someone laughed.

"There is a fire, sir!" Keith shouted at the captain
who was standing aft talking to Mr. Goodfellow.

"A fire!" screamed Captain Mathews and looked
wildly about him.

"In the hold, sir. The forecastle is filled with
smoke."

The captain leaned one arm against the mainmast,
as though he feared falling. "No . . . No . . . It
can't be true." He spoke the words to no one; and for
a moment I felt sorry for him, though beneath my
breath I repeated the old sailor's words.

"We'll all be blown to kingdom come!"

13

"GET THE PUMP RIGGED," the captain screamed.

"The boats, sir. Let's get the boats out first!" cried one of the older sailors.

The captain turned to the tar and bellowed, "Get the pump rigged. If my ship is to be blown up, every man of you shall go with her."

Mr. Goodfellow called for the carpenter, for it was he who tended the pump and was responsible for it being in working order. Old Noah was nowhere to be seen.

"He started the fire," I whispered to Jack who was standing next to me.

"Who?"

"Old Noah, Jack . . . Old Noah started the fire."

Mr. Crane, who had run aft to try to get into the hold, now returned with his eyes all watery from smoke. "Let's get the boats out. And be quick about it, my hearties! Unless you are so eager to get to heaven that you care to be blown up there!"

Our two boats were lying, bottoms up, on the fore hatch. While we loosened the ropes, we could not only smell but see the smoke that drifted through the planks and canvas.

"Take her into the wind!" Mr. Crane cried to the man at the helm.

The breeze was light, and as the *Four Winds* slowly turned her sails backed up. No one thought about the sails. We heard them hit the masts, and did not even bother to look up.

Usually the boats were lowered by running a tackle to one of the yards, but we did not have time for that. We carried the boat to the railing and lifted it over, and let it fall into the sea. We were lucky with the first boat; it landed on its keel, and though it took in a little water, when it hit the sea, it righted itself. Mr. Crane tied the mooring rope of the boat to one of the stays, and ordered the rudder and the oars to be thrown into it.

"Do you think there are sharks?" Mickey Gordon's voice sounded frightened.

Although he had not directed the question to me, I hastened to answer, "I don't think so; they are farther south."

"There ain't none but small sharks here; they eat only children," Jack teased. The excitement in his voice seemed almost gay.

"I ain't afraid," Mickey mumbled, though his heavy lips trembled.

"Everyone get the buckets. No one is abandoning ship before I give the order!" So used were the men to obeying Captain Mathews that those who were carrying the second boat to the railing put it down on the deck.

"Pick up that boat!" This time, it was Mr. Crane who shouted at the men. Confused, the seamen looked from one officer to the other.

"The first man who puts a hand on that boat, I am going to shoot. Now get the buckets and get the pump rigged."

Somehow the sight of the gun in Captain Mathews' hand did not frighten the men, but made them more rebellious. "Let him save his own ship!" one of the sailors cried. The captain glared at him, but he did not shoot.

"Get the boat in the water," Mr. Crane ordered. While he slowly advanced towards the captain, the mate held one of his hands outstretched, palm up, as if he were asking for the revolver.

"This is mutiny, Mr. Crane!" the captain shouted and took a few steps backwards.

"You are wasting our time, sir. You are wasting our lives."

When Mr. Crane came within arm's reach of the gun, the captain fired. The mate turned around as if in a dance, and fell to the deck. The captain looked for a moment at his victim, then at us. I think he was just about to shout an order when he was hit in the shoulder by a marlinspike that Keith the foretopman had thrown at him. The gun fell from Captain Mathews' hand, and Blackie quickly picked it up.

Mr. Goodfellow, who had taken no side in the fight, now ran to the first mate. The captain, holding

his right shoulder with his left hand, hurried aft to his cabin.

"He has another pistol in his cabin. Let's get the boat in the water!" Rolf shouted, and the men followed willingly his order.

Since they had no need of me to help with the boat, I walked over to Mr. Crane. Mr. Goodfellow was holding the first mate's head in his lap. Mr. Crane had been hit in the hip. The deck was red from his blood; but he was still conscious, and when he saw me, he whispered, "Get in the boat, Jim. You are too young to go where I am going." The mate closed his eyes, but he was still smiling, as if the joke had pleased him.

"Get your arms under his other shoulder," Mr. Goodfellow ordered, "and we'll try to carry him."

Mr. Crane moaned as we lifted him up. His right leg hung loosely like a doll's and made a streak of blood across the deck.

The men had not been as lucky with the second boat as they had with the first. It was more than half filled with water, and the top board on the starboard side was smashed, midship. Only Keith the foretopman, Rolf, and Jack had volunteered to board the second boat.

The first, which was the largest of the two boats, drifted a few lengths aft of the *Four Winds*. It was filled to overflowing; and when Mr. Goodfellow ordered the men who manned its oars to come alongside the brig, I feared they would not obey. But the bosun who was at the tiller repeated Mr. Goodfellow's command, and the boat was quickly rowed up to the side of the ship. We let Mr. Crane down by his arms, as gently as we could. Although he fell into the arms of the men below, he cried out in pain.

The smoke was now pouring from the forecastle; and at any minute the fire would reach the powder. Mr. Goodfellow jumped over the railing and into the boat below. I was just about to follow him, when I heard the *meow* of Potiphar.

The cat had sought refuge on the roof of the cook's galley. I ran back to get it, calling its name; but when I approached the frightened animal, it moved towards the center of the roof, so that I had to climb up to catch it. When I returned to the railing with Potiphar in my arms, the longboat had pulled away from the ship and was already far astern. I looked for the second boat; but Keith, Rolf, and Jack, who had thought me safely aboard the longboat, had cut the line of their own sinking boat and were drifting about three boat lengths aft of the brig.

I ran aft to jump overboard and swim after them. I had completely forgotten the captain and old Noah, when I saw a man standing at the helm, staring towards land. At first I thought it was Captain Mathews; but then I recognized the carpenter. His big beard had been singed, and at his temple there was a bloody wound; the blood trickled down his cheek like tears.

I stood beside the old man, yet he did not acknowl-

edge that I was there. Potiphar meowed, and the
shadow of a smile passed over old Noah's face. "The
Lord saveth now with sword and spear: for the battle is the Lord's and He will give you into my hands."

A slight breeze touched his face. The carpenter continued to mumble, but now I could not understand
what he was saying. The damaged boat, with Keith,
Rolf, and Jack aboard, was much too close to the
ship. I pushed the carpenter away from the helm,
and spinning to port I tried to get the *Four Winds*
under way. It was hard work, for I had stuffed the
cat inside my shirt. In his fright, Potiphar was
scratching me, but he did not attempt to escape.

Slowly the brig turned, caught the breeze, and for
the last time, her sails filled out. "Steer her!" I
screamed at the carpenter.

The old man took the wheel from me. "I killed him.
He was a wicked man."

"Yes, sir," I said; then I ran to the railing and leapt
over it.

The water closed over my head, and Potiphar es-
caped from inside my shirt. When I came up to the
surface, the cat was trying to swim towards the burning brig. I grabbed it by the scruff of the neck and
holding one arm above the water, I swam with it.
Had the sea not been as still as it was, I would not
have been able to save the cat. The damaged boat
with my friends in it was about twenty boat lengths
away now. It was my luck that as a child I
had learned to swim in the Avon. Most sailors cannot

swim, and many have been drowned only a few feet away from a boat.

Though the breeze was beginning to die, the *Four Winds* was still sailing; and the carpenter was still standing at the helm. Smoke was pouring from the whole fore part of the ship. Before I reached the boat, I heard the first explosion on board the *Four Winds*. I stopped swimming, and keeping myself afloat by treading water, I watched the ship. It seemed that the whole foredeck had been lifted off. Flames were rising to the top of the mast, making a terrible daylight out of the gloom of evening. Pieces of wood fell near me, but none of them hit me.

It was a great relief to reach the boat and get rid of my passenger. Potiphar never forgave me for saving him.

Rolf pulled me into the boat. "My lad, a cat has seven lives, you have only one."

I looked up at Potiphar, who was already sitting on the aft seat, the only dry place in the boat, busily licking himself. I had risked my life for the cat; but I had done it without thought, as if by instinct — the same instinct that makes you grab the rope when you are working in the rigging.

"Now she blows!" Keith shouted, and I turned to look at the *Four Winds*. The fore part of the ship was one mass of flames, and the foremast was no longer standing; but the aft, oddly enough, was still untouched by the fire, and the mainmast was undamaged. The breeze blew the smoke away from the quarterdeck and I could see old Noah standing at the rudder.

"He killed the captain," I muttered, while I stared at the burning brig.

"Who?" Keith asked.

"Old Noah killed Captain Mathews, he told me he had."

"That's no better than he deserved, the devil!"

I remembered the captain standing before my uncle's desk; though I hated Captain Mathews as much as any of the other men did, the thought that he was no more upset, if it did not sadden, me. That very morning, I had seen him shave. He had worn a blue rag around his neck; and he had cursed Rolf because he claimed that the water I had brought him was not hot.

"She is going!" Jack shouted.

The planks in the waterline of the *Four Winds* had been blown out by the last explosion, and she was drawing water in fast. The flames were dying midship. Suddenly, she turned over on her starboard side, righted herself; and then, slowly the forepart of the ship started on its final voyage, to the bottom of the sea. The aft rose in the air like a burning beacon; and then it too disappeared, and the darkness of the night slapped our faces.

As long as we had had the burning ship as companion, we had not felt alone; nor had we been aware that the evening dusk had turned into night. Now in the darkness, we started to cry "Ahoy!" in the hope that our comrades in the longboat would hear us. After each shout, we waited breathlessly; but only the ripple of the tiny waves against the hull of our water-filled boat answered us.

14

As WE LOST FAITH that our comrades in the longboat could hear us, our cries grew feebler and a strange despair came over us. "They heard us well enough, but they didn't want to share their boat with us," Jack said bitterly.

Rolf shouted a lone "Ahoy"; then he too remained silent.

The child of despair is a hopelessness that can lame even the strongest arm and the most courageous mind. Long we sat in the water-filled boat, saying nothing to each other, feeling apart and lonely. Without warning Keith started to laugh; not hysterically but friendlily, as if he had just thought of a joke that he wanted us all to hear. The darkness in our minds left, and only the darkness of the night remained.

"Let's empty this washtub," he said warmly.

"What with?" Jack asked. "I ain't drinking salt water."

It was true. We had no buckets or anything else that we could bail with.

"With our trousers," Keith answered. None of us understood what he meant until he stripped himself of his trousers, tied knots in each leg, and then started to use them as if they were a bucket.

Once we were doing something to save ourselves, our mood changed; and should a mermaid have heard us, she would have thought we were children on an outing, not shipwrecked sailors. Soon we had gotten enough water out of it to call our tub a boat. Still, had the sea not been almost as still as a lake, we might never have survived; and certainly, had there been any waves to speak of, we could not have sailed. The boat, when new, had had oarlocks for six oars; but on the starboard side only one had not been damaged when the top board was smashed. To make matters worse, we had only two oars and no rudder, so that we had to steer by rowing as well. Rolf sat in the bow, where the one usable oarlock on the starboard side was; and Keith sat midship and rowed on the port side.

When they finally admitted that they were tired, Jack and I relieved them. Whereas Rolf and Keith the foretopman had been of equal strength, Jack was far stronger than I, and the boat constantly was being pulled towards starboard by his more powerful strokes. Every fifth stroke, Jack had to rest, or the boat would have sailed in circles. Soon Keith declared that our rowing was making him seasick, and he took my oar from me. Now Jack had the same trouble as I had had. His oar slipped and he muttered.

Rolf laughed, "My boy, that word your mother didn't teach you."

The night was warm and the breeze gentle; yet few men have longed for the dawn as much as we did. The stars in the dark sky seemed so far away and so lonely; we longed for the sun, for the light, for the sight of land. When finally the eastern sky paled and the stars grew dim, we sat silently and watched the upcoming sun.

"It is there!" Jack cried triumphantly. All of us felt relieved, for though we had not spoken of it, each had had the same fear; namely, that the currents of the ocean could have drawn us away from land. The shore was there, but it seemed as far away as it had

the night before, when last we had gazed upon it.

"Let's row!" Keith started pulling on his oar, and Rolf with a sigh bent his back. Using our shirts, Jack and I mopped up the last of the water in the boat. It had no leaks, and as long as the sea was calm, it was seaworthy.

Potiphar greeted the sunrise with a loud *meow*, which made us smile. The cat was sitting in the rear of the boat like an admiral. "By noon, you'll be catching American mice," I said and stroked him. Potiphar looked up and cocked his head, as if to say, "I remember you, you are the fellow who wanted to drown me."

"One . . . Two . . . One . . . Two . . ." Keith was calling the time as they rowed.

"What about a song, Rolf?" Jack pleaded.

"Not now," Rolf mumbled and went on rowing.

Jack started to sing a song that is often sung when a ship lights anchor:

> *High-ho and up she rises,*
> *High-ho and up she rises*
> *So early in the morning.*

No one joined him and soon he stopped, to sit and glare at the distant shore.

"The sun is our friend . . . It warms us, makes the plants grow, makes an old man content . . . Curse the sun! May the ocean swallow it up and put

out its fire!" Rolf was muttering beneath his breath
as he rowed.

The beat was no longer "One . . . Two . . ." but
"One . . . . . . Two . . . ." It was almost noon; the
sun was burning straight down upon us. I was lying
in the bottom of the boat; my shirt, which I had
drenched in salt water, covered my face. My throat
was parched and I was thinking of wells, of deep
wells with cool water in them. The land seemed as
far away as ever, for now the horizon was engulfed
in a haze of heat. Yet it was the sight of the land —
however blurred — that kept us from sinking again
into despair. That and the knowledge that every man's
courage was linked to all the others like a chain; and
should one link weaken and give way, the chain
would break.

"One . . . Two . . . One . . . Two . . ." I kept mum-
bling to myself. Now I was at the oar. Jack, who was
rowing in the bow, was so tired that he seemed more
my equal in strength. I kept thinking of the cottage
that my mother and I had lived in, when I was a
child, and of the river that flowed near it; for I was
trying to concentrate on pleasant things. Yet every
once in a while, in my mind the ghost of the carpenter would appear. Sternly he would face me with sorrow in his eyes. Who was he? For each man's life is
like a book, a story has been written in it; but few
can read the writing, even when it tells the story of
their own lives. Most men can recall no more than an
incident or two from their childhoods; and these are

more often than not the events that life has written with pain.

"Are we coming any nearer?" Jack called over his shoulder.

I turned around to look at the land, but in the heat of the sun it seemed to have melted into the sea.

"It is only a haze," I asserted, though I did not believe my own words.

"Tomorrow we shall be too tired to row."

I wanted to disagree with Jack, but I couldn't, for I knew that he was right: we must reach land that night.

"Getting tired?" Keith looked up at me. He was lying cross-length at my feet.

"No," I answered; but neither Jack nor I objected when Keith and Rolf relieved us at the oars.

I fell asleep and a strange dream came to me: I was at home, sitting at the table eating supper. My mother was there, but at the head of the table sat a strange man. My mother told me that he was my father. I looked at him earnestly, for I had never known my father, since he had died so soon after I was born. Yet the more I gazed at my father, the more indistinct his face became, until it seemed he had no features at all. "Mother," I cried, "he has no face." My mother laughed at me, telling me to look again. I did, and this time I recognized the man sitting at the head of the table; it was old Noah, the carpenter.

I must have screamed or gasped in my sleep, for

Rolf grabbed my shoulder and shook me. "What's the matter, Jim?"

When I looked into Rolf's face, I could not help smiling; he looked at once both concerned and a little frightened. "You were screaming. Did you have a nightmare?"

I nodded; then I contradicted myself by shaking my head, for was it a nightmare? If the ghost of the carpenter wanted to haunt me in my dreams, then it would be best for me to make a friend of him. Old Noah was a man to whom the world had done much injustice; of this I was certain. "An orphan of the wind," I thought. A moment later, I said it aloud to Rolf. "Old Noah was an orphan of the wind." Rolf smiled compassionately, and I believe he understood.

It was much cooler. I turned about and looked towards the west. The haze was gone; the low marsh land was not far away!

"Land!" I exclaimed.

Jack was beside me laughing. "You were right, it was only a haze!" I laughed, too, for when I had spoken of the haze, I had been convinced that we would never reach land, that our boat would be our coffin.

The Face of Peace

15

"So THIS IS AMERICA!" Keith looked up and down the beach that stretched white in the moonlight. "Nobody here to welcome us!"

Jack bent down and picked up some sand, then let it fall through his fingers. "Poor soil for potatoes."

"But better than the sea," Rolf said. "As soon as it is light, we must try to get inland."

We stretched ourselves out on the sand. I was sure that I could not sleep; yet so tired was I, that I had hardly finished wording the thought before sleep had come.

We were awakened by rain. Fresh water that ran down our faces and into our mouths and helped quench our thirst. The rain storm did not last; it was gone as suddenly as it had come. Yet it had not only refreshed our parched lips and throats, but it had made us feel that luck was with us; and sailors — aye, and most other people too — are superstitious, and if they have lost faith in their luck, they will give up. In spite of our damp clothing, we fell asleep again, and did not wake until the sun was shining brightly down on us.

Jack pointed north, along the seemingly unending beach. "All we have to do is walk northwest, and we

come to a town called New York, and there we can
join the Union Army."

Rolf and Keith the foretopman laughed. None of
us had moved from the spot on which he had slept.
"It isn't so easy, young friend. America is a big country, and you will wear your legs off to your knees before you get to New York." Rolf stood up, and looking
east towards the sea, he squinted his eyes as he stared
into the face of the sun. "All you have to do is swim
northeast, then you come to a town called Bristol,
and when you get there, you just go to a tavern, called
The Hangman's Folly and tell the barmaid that Rolf
sent you."

"There is no such tavern as The Hangman's Folly in
Bristol."

"So young and yet he knows all the public houses

in Bristol," Keith remarked. Soon Jack and Keith
were wrestling good-naturedly on the sand. Keith
was much stronger than Jack and quickly pinned him
down. When they both rose, Jack looked at me. I
laughed, for I had guessed his thoughts. When Jack
had thrown me down on the sand, quite as easily as
Keith had thrown him, we started to discuss seriously
what we ought to do.

"We must have food and water. We don't know
how long the beach is, nor where it ends. If we can
make our way through the marsh to solid land, we
will find people living there."

"But they will be slavers," I interrupted Keith.

"And so will we be!"

Rolf's remark surprised me, as it did Jack, but not
Keith the foretopman; he nodded in agreement.

"None of you has any opinions on slavery," Rolf
explained, "and if you do, then you are for it."

Jack wrinkled his nose and shrugged his shoulders,
and by these mute gestures expressed his opinion of
Rolf's advice.

"In time of war, people don't have opinions, only
nations do. War not only kills men, but it shackles
their minds, as well. That's why lots of men like war;
it saves them from having to think." Rolf's voice was
bitter.

Only a month ago, I would not have understood
what he meant, but now I did. Growing up is not like
a walk up a hill; it is like climbing a precipice, and
every so often having to look down.

Keith, who was much younger than Rolf, was more able to cope with Jack's displeasure. "We must be like spies; and maybe something we will see will be of use to the people in the north."

This idea appealed at once to Jack; for, next to being a pirate, there is nought so romantic as a spy. I watched Jack smile in his enthusiastic agreement; and I thought to myself, You may be stronger than I am, but I am cleverer. And now I did not mind that he had won over me so easily when we wrestled.

We could not walk through the marsh, for it was more water than it was land, and tall reeds grew in it. The water was brackish and unfit for drinking; and it was much warmer than the sea. A short distance south of our landing place, we found a canal through the reeds.

"This is our path," Rolf said and Keith nodded. Jack objected that we had no boat. Our own boat we could not possibly carry across the beach; we had only managed with the greatest of our combined strengths to draw it halfway out of the sea.

"We will build a raft," Keith said, and ordered Jack and me to collect large pieces of driftwood, while he and Rolf continued to explore the beach by walking north.

It was a long time before we had enough timber for a raft. Although there was much driftwood to be found, little of it was usable: some pieces were too large; more than a few were too small; others that were the right size were too rotten. We found two pieces of a main yard, which the four of us together carried to our "shipyard." These made up the frame of our raft and gave it buoyancy. The driftwood that Jack and I had gathered became the deck. In our abandoned boat, there was fourteen feet of line, and along the beach we found bits of rope; with them we tied the pieces of wood onto the heavy logs. By late morning we had a seaworthy raft, large enough to accommodate the four of us.

We were about to push off, when a loud *meow* from Admiral Potiphar reminded us that he was still on the beach. We had not seen the cat all morning. We called to Potiphar, and he came. He sniffed at the raft, and then jumped aboard.

The wood had been well dried. The raft lay high in the water; its deck was dry. Using our oars to punt with, we started on the final part of our "voyage."

Soon we were in a world of reeds. Sometimes the canal was broad, and our oars could hardly reach the bottom, so we had to use them as paddles. Other times, it would grow narrow and shallow; and we would have to push the reeds apart to make our way forward.

Several times, the canal divided itself, and we had to judge which was the better route. Once we made a mistake and we had to double back when the canal ended in a reed forest. We did not see many birds, but we heard them. Once a dolphin glided by us, giving us a greeting from the sea that we had left behind,

and telling us that somewhere the canal was directly
connected with the ocean.

In the middle of the afternoon, we found an island.
On it some low trees were growing. By then we were

very hungry and extremely thirsty. Our eyes were a little swollen. Keith and Rolf with their unshaven beards looked like a couple of highwaymen. We had been in our work clothes when we had had to abandon ship, and I had taken off my canvas shoes before I had jumped overboard.

I think Potiphar saw the house first, for he unexpectedly meowed loudly, stretched himself, and got up from his place in the center of the raft. It was a strange house, built at the edge of the canal, with a porch that rested on wooden poles, running the full length of the house. If we were amazed by the sudden appearance of a house — we had just rounded a bend in the canal — I am sure the man sitting on the porch in his rocking chair, with a fishing pole in his hand, was even more so. There we were: four dirty men, dressed in clothes that were hardly more than rags, with a cat, on a primitive raft.

"Ahoy!" he cried, probably because he felt that a maritime greeting was fitting.

"Ahoy," we answered; but we did not know what to say beyond that.

The man drew in his fishing line. "Where are you going?"

"To the Indies," answered Keith the foretopman. "Are we sailing in the right direction?"

"You're a little off course." He paused and then he added gaily, "Your name is Christopher Colombus, I presume."

It was a funny introduction; but it made the best impression possible on Mr. Anthony, who, as we quickly learned, was very fond of a joke. He was the overseer on a large estate, on the Island of Edisto. He, his wife, and their two daughters were the only white residents on the whole island.

At first it was a little difficult for us to understand our hosts, especially Mrs. Anthony, for the people of the American south speak English very softly, and so slowly that it seems as if they hate to part with each word, so they draw out the saying of it as long as possible. Fortunately, it was not until after we had washed and Rolf and Keith had shaved that we were required to converse very much.

"Three days! That's how long they held out, then Major Anderson had to draw the flag. I am telling you all, it won't be long before our troops have captured Washington, and New York, too!"

None of us contradicted Mr. Anthony, for we were at the table eating. It seemed not only bad manners to disagree with our benefactor, but foolish as well.

"Now, how about the English helping us?"

Rolf put down the leg of chicken that he had been gnawing on, but before he could swallow what was already in his mouth, so that he could speak, Jack started to answer. I say "started" to answer, for he never got farther than "I don't think any — " when Keith kicked him under the table. I was sitting next to Jack, and I am sure the blow must have hurt a good

deal. Jack said no more for the rest of the meal. But though he had lost the desire to tell what he thought his countrymen wanted to do about the American Civil War, his appetite revived at once and he gladly concentrated on eating.

"I am sure that Queen Victoria will do the right thing," Rolf finally mumbled.

"That is what I reckon, too," said Mr. Anthony and beamed at us.

"France, too, will come to our aid. They need our cotton. I will say, for sure, that this here little war won't last the summer out; then that fool in the White House can go to Africa and live."

"What is the name of the President?" Keith asked. I noticed that his mouth was greasy, and I suspected that he had eaten two chickens, by himself.

"Jefferson Davis, my boy."

Keith looked confused, as did Rolf. It seemed to me, too, that I had heard the name of the American President, and though I could not recall it, I felt certain that the name Mr. Anthony had mentioned was not the President's.

"And that is the fellow you are going to send to Africa?" the foretopman asked.

"Jefferson Davis is the name of the President of the Confederate States of America. He is a southern gentleman! The man who is now in the White House — you can call it the Black House, if you want to — is named Abraham Lincoln. He is a lawyer from

the west, that had to run east because he had taken
all his clients' money."

Mr. Anthony was a good-natured man, and we
were to hear much worse things about Mr. Lincoln,
on our way north, than that he was merely dishonest.

On Edisto there was no war, only talk of it. The
trees bowed gently in the breeze; the crickets and
the frogs sang. After dinner, we four were outside alone, which was just as well, for Keith and Jack
were both nauseous, nor was I feeling much better
than they. "That's what you get for being greedy,"
Rolf said.

"Why did you kick me in the shin, Keith?" Jack
asked.

"Because you were sitting on the part I wanted to
kick," the foretopman answered with a grin.

"Sirs!" The voice came from behind us, and we
were startled, for we thought we were alone in the
dusk. It was an elderly Negro who addressed us. His
closely curled hair was gray and he was wearing a
white jacket. At dinner, he had waited on us. "Sir,
Master told me to tell you that coffee would be served
on the porch."

I am sure we stared at him — probably rather
rudely. Finally, Jack said, "Would you mind saying
that first word again?"

The Negro was perplexed; nonetheless, he replied,
"The first word I said was 'Sirs.'"

Jack pulled at his ears and pretended to clean them with his forefingers. "I just ain't used to it. It's the first time that anyone has ever called this jack tar, 'sir.'"

"Yes, sir," the Negro said softly.

"What do you think of that fellow Jefferson Davis?" Keith the foretopman asked the slave.

"I don't know any Master Jefferson Davis," the Negro answered, and he looked at Keith a little apprehensively.

Keith grinned, patted the old man on the shoulder, and walked past him towards the porch. Later, he said to Jack and me, "The slave didn't dare say anything in front of us, and I don't blame him either."

"Now your Queen, she is a lady, and it would be natural for her to side with us, out of chivalry."

It was late. Outside, the night was dark; but Mr. Anthony, who seldom had visitors, kept on talking. He spoke to us as if we knew the Queen personally and as if he, himself, were a close friend of Jefferson Davis. Once he even said "Jeff."

Slowly the words of Mr. Anthony faded, as though a door had silently been closed. I had fallen asleep in my chair. Suddenly my head, which had been resting against the back of the chair, fell forward. I woke with a start, and almost tumbled out of the chair.

"The young gentleman is sleepy."

I wondered whom Mr. Anthony could be talking

about, for, just as Jack was unused to being called
"Sir," I had never before been referred to as a gentleman.

Jack and I were led to a room with a strange little
window that was near the floor, through which we
could see the forest of reeds. We slept until noon, yet
when we opened our eyes we wanted to remain in
bed. We were still tired, and the clean sheets against
our bodies felt so nice.

"Everybody out of his bunk!" Keith's smiling face
was looking at us from the open door. Jack pulled
the covers up over his head; but Keith quickly tipped
his bed and he fell to the floor.

Downstairs in the parlor, we found Rolf deep in
conversation with Mr. Anthony; and for a moment,
I wondered if either of them had gone to bed at all.

"Now the way I figure it, we in the south naturally
know how to treat the black man. We have lived
with them; they are like our children. I don't hold with
any mistreatment. Why, a man who has to beat Negroes or children ain't a proper man in my eyes."

Rolf looked at us pleadingly and then remarked
uncomfortably, "But, sir, do you think that the
slaves agree with you?"

"Most of them do, that I swear to you! Why, they
are like our children. If any of them gets sick, I send
for the Charleston doctor. You won't see any mistreatment here!"

Rolf shrugged his shoulders, which Mr. Anthony
noticed. "Over in England, you are all white. I sup-

pose you don't notice when you read the Bible that
it says right there that the sons of Ham shall work the
fields."

Many a time before we reached the north we would
hear this argument; but it did not influence me, for I
am certain that the Good Lord knew well enough the
hearts of Adam's descendants not to give them slaves.
The Lord who told us to love our fellowman as ourselves just couldn't lead us purposely into temptation.
Many things can be discussed. I'll admit many sides
to most questions; but there are some things in life
that one must not doubt. Man is as man does; the
color of his skin is of no more importance than the
color of his eyes.

Yet Mr. Anthony was kind, which shows how difficult it is to judge men. What parted him and Rolf
was merely an opinion, a belief; their hearts were
equally pure. But so strong can a belief be that it
can turn a good person into a man capable of doing
evil. Kind Mr. Anthony, who willingly would do no
man injustice, would defend — yes, go to war to
defend! — the rights of the slaveholder: the right of
the whip, the right to sell children away from their
mothers.

I am sure that most of the slaves on Edisto loved
Mr. Anthony. When you are born a slave and freedom is but a dream, all you can pray for is a kind
master. Kindness can sweeten the bitter wine of injustice, it can lighten the shackles of slavery, but it
is no substitute for justice or freedom.

Four days we stayed on Edisto. Four days in which we enjoyed peace, for Mr. Anthony got tired of talking about war. His real interests were fishing, hunting, and the farm, which in these warm climates is called a plantation. He grew many vegetables that we had never seen before, and we tasted fruits we had never heard of. Rolf called the island the Garden of Eden. So it was, and we would have stayed much longer, if the snake had not appeared.

Early the morning of the fourth day of our visit, the owner of the plantation arrived. He was a small, thin man, with wisps of yellow hair on his head. His name was Williams, Mr. William Williams. He claimed that his family had come from England over a hundred years ago to settle on Edisto — which probably is true, but it is not a credit to either country. He reminded me of my uncle. He was petty. He could not have killed a man, as old Noah or Captain Mathews could; yet he could torment his neighbor for the sake of an extra shilling.

Inadvertently, he brought us good news. The longboat, with the rest of the crew of the *Four Winds,* had arrived safely in Charleston. Eagerly, we plied him with questions about Mr. Crane. He replied that he thought the man must be alive, for there had been no mention of anyone on the longboat being dead; but his answer was given so impatiently that we knew it could not matter to him what happened to Mr. Crane or anyone else with whom he was not directly connected.

Mr. Williams told us that there would be berths
for us in the Confederate Navy, for though the southern states had few ships, they had fewer trained men
than they needed. Ill-temperedly, he added that if we
did not go at once to Charleston and enlist we would
be arrested; and that he had no intention of harbor-
ing us on his property. Then when he appeared convinced that his threats had intimidated us, he spoke
of the "glories of the south," and the "evil of the north";
but only when he spoke of the Abolitionists, who
stole other men's property, did his eyes gleam.

I had never heard of the Abolitionists; and it was

some time before I realized that the "property" he was talking about was slaves. If the kindness of Mr. Anthony had blunted in our minds the tragedy of being born a slave, Mr. Williams' arguments brought the horror and the pain once more to the fore.

"No chance that I berth on one of those ships," someone mumbled. I turned to look at Jack; but it was Keith the foretopman who had whispered aloud his conviction. The expression on Rolf's face was, if anything, more eloquent than Keith's hushed protest.

Mr. Williams' thin lips grew thinner. He told us that he was reporting our existence to the military command.

Mrs. Anthony had prepared a huge basket of food for us; and Mr. Anthony gave me a new pair of canvas shoes, and Keith a shirt, for his own was torn past repairing.

We felt ashamed when we said good-bye to the Anthonys. Mr. Anthony wished us luck in the navy; he said that he was sure that Rolf would become an officer. Again and again, we thanked him for his kindness.

For me there was the further sadness in leaving Edisto that I had to leave Potiphar as well. I had argued with Rolf that I could carry the cat; but he had only laughed and remarked that the mice on Edisto would do very well for Admiral Potiphar. Maybe my love for the cat showed that I was still a child, for children love animals with a passion that grownups cannot understand. I think it is because children are nearer to being animals themselves; and nearer, too, to the fairy-tale world in which animals speak and a toad may be a bewitched princess. As for Potiphar, we had journeyed with *him*, not he with us. If we foolishly wanted to travel on, well . . . He gave us a last *meow*, then licked his paw and stretched himself in the warm sunshine.

16

"Listen, Jim" — Keith looked at me while he rubbed his feet — "should anyone ever tell you that the United States of America is not a big country, you just call him a barefaced liar."

I nodded. Rolf laughed and bent down to examine the water in the brook. We had been resting there for almost an hour. "Won't be any fish in this brook for the next ten years, they'll die of poison. Interesting color your feet have, Jim. Remember to wash them before you go to bed tonight or you'll get the sheets dirty." Everyone laughed, even myself, while Rolf splashed with his own poorman's horses. I wiggled my toes, rubbed some of the dirt off my feet, and then stuck them back into the cool water.

It was five days since we had left Edisto. We had walked about twenty-five miles a day. At night, we slept in fields, or if luck was with us, in a haystack. Food was not too difficult to get, for we told farmers' wives that we were on our way to join the Confederate Army. To avoid meeting the recruiting sergeant, we walked around all the larger towns. We were not lonely on the roads; small companies of soldiers marched by us. The officers were in the gray uniforms

of the Army of the Confederate States, but the men
for the most part wore work clothes and carried their
rifles as if they were pitchforks. Not only soldiers, but
also ordinary people were on the move; and everyone seemed gay, as if it were a party he was hurry-
ing to.

Shortly after we left the brook, we passed a company of soldiers who were singing. Rolf, as he gazed
at their happy faces, said, "Aye, these boys dance
at their own funerals."

Yet I must admit that Keith, Jack, and myself were
not much different; for us, too, tomorrow was far
away. When, later that afternoon, we came to a
large village, we insisted upon entering it; carefree
we laughed at Rolf's warnings. When we arrived at
the village green, a Colonel of the Confederate Cav-
alry was standing on a roughly made wooden platform
giving a speech. We were frightened, but realizing
that we would have made ourselves more conspicu-
ous by going on, we joined the large crowd.

The officer was tall, slenderly built, and wore the
handsomest uniform I have ever seen. Not that the
material was so extraordinary, but the gold on the
sleeves seemed to be real gold, and his yellow cap
was made of velvet. Many of the uniforms we had
seen until now had appeared homemade, but this one
must have been fitted by a tailor. The colonel spoke
beautifully. His speech was addressed to the "Wives,
mothers, and sweethearts of our soldiers . . ."

"If the devil ever needs an advocate, I'll have a

suggestion for him," Keith whispered to Rolf, loud enough for me to hear him.

Rolf grumbled, "He ate honey and washed it down with perfume, before he started that speech."

"He is going to take up a collection soon," Keith continued.

"He is just like Vicar Hunter at home, when he talks about the orphans on Christmas Eve," Jack whispered.

In front of the speaker was a large box draped in a Confederate flag. Standing at attention beside it, was a young man, who, had he been only an inch or two shorter, would have been called a midget; he was dressed in a sergeant's uniform. To his rifle was fixed a bayonet, which — because of the man's abnormally small size — appeared enormous.

As Keith and Jack had predicted, the orator soon made an appeal for financial aid to "our new government." The crowd quickly began to thin out as it always does on such occasions when approval more tangible than applause or a hearty hurrah is requested. Some people, however, did drop money in the box; there were especially many women among the donators; and to each the colonel himself gave a soulful glance and mumbled his thanks.

If we had left the village common at this point, all might have been saved, but we lingered on; even Rolf did not hear the beating of the drums in the distance that announced the arrival of a recruiting officer. The drums were beaten by two Negroes; behind them marched a captain and a sergeant, who were followed by a dozen young men. The new recruits were cheered by the crowd as soon as they came into view, and they in turn yelled flattering remarks about the girls in the crowd.

"They are recruiting . . . Let's run!" Jack whispered desperately.

We looked about us. We were standing alone. The crowd had moved towards the recruiting officer, who was only now approaching the common. The platform was deserted. The midget sergeant, with the money box under his arm, was walking across the broad lawn, in the opposite direction from the newcomers; and the colonel in the elegant uniform was out of sight.

It was too late for us to run; the recruiting officer with long, quick strides was approaching the platform. As he climbed up, the Negroes stopped their incessant beating of the drums. The captain looked about himself nervously and shifted his weight from one leg to the other. When he did at last manage to glance directly at his audience, he stepped backwards.

"Looks like he was driving a mule team," an old man said loudly, and several people snickered.

The captain's speech lasted no more than a few minutes; and judging from the sweat on his forehead, these minutes were as long for him as they had been for his audience. But when he was finished there was a rousing cheer.

"Even a deaf-mute could get an ovation here," Keith said. "All he has to do is wave the flag."

Unfortunately for us, the recruiting officer's declamatory powers were not the measure of his efficiency. Suddenly we realized that everyone was staring at us, while from the platform the captain was pointing in our direction.

"Attention!" screamed Keith the foretopman. "Line up!"

In spite of our confusion, we obeyed him, for we knew not what else to do. The three of us formed a line and awaited further instructions.

"Right turn, forward march!" Keith shouted as loud as a battle-trained sergeant.

At first we did not know where Keith was leading us. Along the side of the road, which led out of the town towards the north, there was a bright new carriage, with two chestnut-colored horses harnessed to it, that appeared just about to depart. When we came within twenty yards of it, we recognized the midget sergeant sitting on the box in front, with the reins in his hands.

The colonel stuck his head out of the carriage window and looked at us in astonishment. Keith ordered us to halt and walked up to the carriage alone. The colonel stepped out and Keith saluted him smartly.

We had to read the content of Keith's conversation with the colonel in the face of that well-dressed officer, for the foretopman spoke too softly for us to hear him. At first, the southerner looked at Keith with such loathing that one might have supposed our comrade to be President Lincoln himself; but then a smile lurked at his mouth. Finally, he nodded in agreement to whatever it was Keith had suggested. Keith saluted most militarily for a tar, and the colonel returned to his carriage.

"Fall in, in pairs!" Keith shouted.

"We are only three soldiers, General," Jack replied very sarcastically.

"I want no mutiny here. I'll have you taste the cat!" Then, as if he suddenly had become even angrier, Keith added threateningly, "I'll have you keel-hauled through the fleet. Rolf, fall in with Jim, and you, Jack, fall in behind them."

Jack was about to protest again when a low "Shut up!" from Rolf made him obey Keith's orders.

We marched: Keith in front, Rolf and I beside each other, and Jack bringing up the rear. The sergeant on the box looked back to make sure we were behind the carriage; then he flipped the whip and steered the carriage to port, down the road which led out of the village. The entire crowd was now close at hand; they had watched the military exercise with great interest; and now they applauded and screamed to cheer us on our way. I wanted to turn around and look at them, but glancing sideways I saw Rolf's face. He was looking so sternly forward that I dared not look back.

We marched about a mile behind the carriage; then, when the road turned and the village was hidden from view — or rather, when we were hidden from the villagers' view — the colonel ordered the carriage to halt. He stepped out of it, beckoned to Keith to approach him, and then to our astonishment handed the foretopman several coins. Keith saluted, but the handsome officer did not return his salute. He returned to his seat in the carriage and roughly ordered the sergeant to drive on. The midget whipped the horses forward and the carriage soon disappeared behind a hill.

We three — Rolf, Jack, and I — turned inquisitively to Keith, who was proudly counting the money. "I knew he was no soldier. I haven't sailed on two of Her Majesty's frigates for nothing. I know officers from tigers to monkeys."

Rolf shook his head, as if he had seen a miracle.

"But what was he?"

"I think he was an actor," Keith replied.

"And so are you!" I blurted, as I looked up at Keith with admiration.

"There's eight dollars," Keith announced happily. Jack was so jubilant that he started to dance. Rolf, however, looked gloomy; and as the rest of us became aware of his mood, ours too changed.

"I don't hold with slavers, nor with their war," he began thoughtfully. "But the man who fights for a bad cause is more decent than he who seeks to make profit out of a good one. Those who profit from this war are worse than the slavers who sell their fellow-men into slavery and suffering; for they —" and he stretched his arm out in the direction in which the false colonel had gone — "they who profit from wars, profit from death!"

"Here, take the money," Keith said solemnly and handed Rolf the coins, but the cook let them fall into the dust.

Quickly Jack picked the money up and stuffed it in his pockets. "No reason when bad money comes to good men, they should throw it away."

Rolf's brow was furrowed. He held out his hand towards Jack. Reluctantly, Jack took the money from his pockets and handed it to the cook.

"We aren't in the north yet; maybe that money was meant for us to get there with," I said softly to Rolf. "We are orphans of the wind, maybe the colonel was sent to help us."

Rolf shoved the money into his pocket. "A rat can always find a rat hole, but it is hard for an honest man to squeeze into one to save his skin."

"You sound like the carpenter," Keith said bitterly, and I realized that none of us had thanked him for saving us from the recruiting officer. "A tar must take his luck where he can find it."

As I turned to look at Rolf, I remembered old Noah, and it seemed that Keith's accusation was true. The cook's face was as stern as the carpenter's had been, nor did Rolf laugh as often or as heartily as he used to.

As if to give the lie to my thoughts, Rolf suddenly laughed and put his arm about my shoulders; then he grabbed hold of Jack; and the three of us followed Keith the foretopman down the road.

17

"THOSE WHEELS ought to be greased."

What Jack had said was true; the wheels of the wagon we walked beside whined like a whipped dog, but I was too tired to care.

"If there ain't anything else, you can use hog fat to grease the axle with," Jack continued.

I almost mumbled aloud the absurd thought that came into my mind about lard being a cure for chilblains; but fortunately I remembered it was July and that the torments of chilblains came only in winter. It was probably because my feet ached so terribly that I had thought about chilblains.

The wagon stopped, and I looked ahead to see what was the matter. The soldiers, as far as I could see, had stopped marching. "What's the matter?" I asked Jack, though I knew the question was foolish, for how could Jack know why a halt had been ordered, any more than I did.

"It's the enemy, they've attacked," he replied gaily.

"I don't hear any firing." In a whisper I added, "Aren't we the enemy? I mean this being the Confederate Army?"

Jack grinned. "The Yankees have shot General

Johnston and now we have all got to go on parade for
his funeral."

For more than a week we had been traveling with
the Confederate Army, commanded by General
Johnston. We were doing chores in the field kitchen
belonging to a regiment from South Carolina, under
the command of Captain Hines. It had been Rolf's
idea that it would be far easier to hide *in* the southern
army than *from* it. At times we cursed Rolf, for we
had to work hard; still — as Rolf had predicted — we
had moved north rapidly and soon would be near the
Union Army. Our plan was to escape and join them,
as soon as possible.

"What's the matter?" asked Keith the foretopman,
as he approached Jack and me. He and Rolf followed
a cart farther back in the line.

"I don't know," I answered, "but Jack thinks it's
the Yankees attacking."

Keith laughed loudly. "There ain't no such thing
as Yankees. We will march all the way to Canada; and
by that time we will have worn our legs off to the
knees; but we won't see any Yankees."

The soldiers in front of us began to move. Slowly
they dragged themselves forward.

"Look there," Keith said as he pointed ahead. "It's
a railroad. Let's go and buy tickets to the nearest battle."

The station house was near the road; there was a
sign above it which read: "Manassas Junction." Here

two railway lines joined, but there was no town, only a lonely farmhouse and the station. The wagon shook and rattled as the mules pulled it across the track.

Halfway across, one of the wheels of the wagon parted from its axle and rolled on alone until it fell into a ditch. It was a rear wheel, and the wagon hobbled on for a few feet on three wheels, then it fell over on its side. The mules kept pulling it forward, as if nothing had happened, and before the driver managed to stop them, the turned-over wagon blocked the road.

"What's the matter?" the sergeant in charge of the kitchen yelled as he ran forward.

The driver, who seldom spoke, merely pointed to the wheel which was lying in the ditch. Somehow, the wheel resting there alone at the roadside looked to me as if it were dead. The sergeant mopped his brow with a large handkerchief, which once must have been white, and gazed unhappily at the wheel.

"What's the matter?" A lieutenant on horseback looked angrily at the sergeant, who grimaced at the driver.

"The wheel came off, sir," Keith answered politely, touching his hat as he did so.

"How the ——— did that happen?" the lieutenant screamed at Keith, as though he was convinced that Keith was responsible for the accident.

I felt an arm around my shoulder and realized that Rolf had joined us.

"I am a sailor, sir," Keith explained, "and I don't know much about wagons, but I think that the axle's broken."

The lieutenant looked at the wagon and then at us.

"What's holding us up?" Captain Hines, who was walking towards us, was a thin man, with a bitter expression on his face; but he was not an incompetent officer. Before the lieutenant had a chance to explain what had happened, the captain ordered the mules to be unharnessed and the five of us — the driver, Jack, Keith, Rolf, and myself — to pull the wagon to the side of the road.

"You four stay here with the driver and help him. When you have got the wagon repaired, then follow us."

"Aye, sir," Keith said and we all saluted. As soon as the officers and the sergeant were out of sight, we sat down in the ditch and watched the regiment pass.

"That lieutenant," Rolf began, "he never thought that a broken wagon could hold up an army. A colorful uniform, the blare of a trumpet, and then victory with the enemy running before him like so many rabbits; that's his idea of war."

When the last of the soldiers had disappeared behind a hill, and the dust had settled on the now empty road, the landscape took on again the character of peace. We could hear a cow lowing to its calf and a dog bark on a nearby farm.

A man was approaching us from the direction of the farm. For a long time he stood silently staring at the wheel in the ditch; then he spit out the piece of straw he had been chewing on. "Better get the wagon unloaded."

The driver, who before he became a soldier had been a farmer, spit on the road in a comradely fashion and smiled.

"Couldn't repair it with all that stuff in it," the stranger continued.

"It's an old wagon," the driver said, as he started to take one of the large sacks of flour off of it.

Working together, within a short time, we had all the kitchen supplies stacked along the roadside.

"Got to get a new axle," the farmer commented slowly.

"You got one?" the driver asked, and glanced at him out of the corners of his eyes.

"Can't say I got one." The farmer was looking at his shoes.

"We could pay you," the driver said softly.

The stranger nodded, though he did not look up. "Still, I would like to help." His neck reddened as he said these words. Keith laughed, but our driver frowned at the foretopman.

"A bag of flour, in these times, is worth more than money," the driver said, and turned to try to catch the farmer's glance.

The stranger bent down, picked a blade of grass, and put it between his teeth. "It ain't new the one I got, but I reckon it will fit."

The driver looked about him, over the green

wooded hills, and then started to walk towards the farmhouse with the farmer at his heels.

"'Everyone gets what he deserves,' as the newly commissioned captain said when he ordered his whole crew flogged," Keith said with a grin, as we watched the retreating backs of the two men.

It was late afternoon by the time the wagon was repaired and we could move on. The road ran through a valley, in which many well-fed cattle grazed; on our right, we passed two farmhouses; then the road divided. The driver halted the wagon and looked about him; there was no one to ask which way Captain Hines' regiment had gone. He scratched his head and looked from one to the other of the equally dusty roads.

"Maybe we can smell which way they went," Keith said and drew the breath in sharply through his nostrils.

The driver took the road branching to the right. With a stick he hit the mules. "Ten points to starboard, the admiral commands," Keith shouted. Like so many other sailors, he disliked farmers and often teased the driver.

We had only walked a little more than a mile, when we caught up not only with our regiment, but with what seemed to us to be the whole southern army, as well.

"You, boys, just hang on with me, and you'll soon be in Washington," the sergeant said jubilantly, when he saw us. He was busy setting up his kitchen in an orchard belonging to a farm. Pointing to the farm-house, he exclaimed, "Do you know who's in there?"

We all turned towards the comfortable looking house. "Abraham Lincoln?" Jack suggested with an insolent smile on his face.

The sergeant was not to be insulted. "General Beauregard!" he said proudly.

"Never heard of him," Jack remarked off-handedly. This was a lie, for there was not one of us who had not heard of the general, who was called the "hero of Fort Sumter."

One of the soldiers who was standing nearby be-gan to curse us all as foreigners; and only Rolf's scold-ing of Jack, which he accompanied by a long expla-nation of General Beauregard's accomplishments and virtues, saved us from having to fight.

The sergeant smiled at Rolf and complimented him for his knowledge. We all liked the sergeant, even though he worked us quite hard and his temper sometimes could be easily aroused. He was not unkind, but he was one of those persons who never doubts. It is doubt that makes a man reef his sails at the first appearance of black clouds on the horizon. He was like so many other southerners we had met; his view was hemmed in by the fair winds that blew for the south at present. As Keith said, "If you have to round Cape Horn, don't shout too joyously about the fair winds in the Channel."

That night, when most of the other men were sleep-ing, we held council. The northern armies were not

far away. Below the farm was a little river called
Bull Run. Beyond the hills on the other side of it were
the Union forces — at least, so we had been told.

It was the twentieth day of July. We decided that
on the following evening or night, we would try to
flee. First we would walk south, then east to cross the
river; and finally, north until we found the northern
army. We spoke of our plan as if it were as easy as a
Sunday's walk, for we all knew the dangers too well
to speak of them aloud. We could be caught by a
southern patrol. The northern army might fire on us
before we had any chance to explain who we were;
or they might mistake us for spies. In war, fear is the
father of most actions.

The ground seemed unusually hard that night, and
we slept very little. When the sky began to grow light,
we rose and started the kitchen fires. Most of the soldiers had slept poorly too. Their faces were drawn
and there was little real laughter.

"We should have slipped out last night," Rolf whispered, and none of us disagreed with him.

When the sun rose, the men came to the kitchen
wagons to get their bread and chicory. Some of them
tried to joke. But the jokes of war are different from
those of peace; and their jokes were still peacetime
jokes, jokes of the barracks. Suddenly, overnight, many
had become aware that bullets can tear the flesh and
stop the heart from beating. Only a few laughed and
there was no heartiness in their laughter.

We all looked towards the farmhouse, the headquarters of General Beauregard. It belonged to a farmer named McLean. The kitchen fire was blazing, smoke curled from the chimney. Every few minutes an officer would walk outside, and one of the soldiers would tell us his name with awe. In that house, our destinies were being shaped. Maps were being studied, maps of fields that soon would be the graves of many of us.

I heard the whistling sound and managed to say "What is that noise?" before the shell struck the kitchen of the farmhouse.

For a moment the explosion seemed to shake the earth. In the silence that followed, I heard Rolf's voice. "That, my boy, was the sound of battle!"

The Reddest Rose

18

The reddest rose
Is the rose of death.

THESE TWO LINES I kept repeating to myself, though the song they came from was about a girl who died because her lover had left her, and had nothing to do with war. I was lying on a hill with a group of soldiers from General Jackson's brigade. It was nearly noon, and I had not seen Jack, or Keith, or Rolf, for several hours. From the hill, there was a view of the valley with the stone bridge over the river, and a small house to the left of it. In my hand I had a rifle. I had fired it twice over the heads of the Union soldiers; yet the very act of firing had brought me a strange feeling of security in the midst of battle.

In battle I had been, and so had my three comrades, for we had had no choice. If we had tried to run away, or stay behind, when the order had been given for our regiment to march towards Henry House Hill (to join General Jackson's brigade), we would have been shot as deserters. We were not the only soldiers who did not wear proper uniforms. Some, like the 33rd Virginia, even wore the blue uniforms of the Union Army.

All morning the regiment had been engaged. This was our first respite, and I was looking about me to see if I could catch a glimpse of one of my comrades. With horror I realized that a man lying near me was dead; his mouth was open as if he had died screaming. At the outset, the four of us had tried to stay together, but in the confusion we quickly lost each other. For this I tell you: battle and confusion are the same words. It is like a full-rigged ship, with all sails set, suddenly hit by a storm. For the last hour or two, we had been retreating, farther and farther up the hill. The officers shouted orders at us, but who understood what was said? As everyone else, I followed the man in front of me, and hoped I would not be hit. If one man had thrown down his rifle and fled, hundreds would have followed him. If one had charged and run against the enemy, he would find himself leading a regiment. So close in battle is victory to defeat. General Jackson who commanded us had courage to waste; and truly, was it not wasted? Brothers fighting brothers; men of virtue like General Jackson defending the most despicable of all institutions, slavery?

"I shot someone!" It was Jack, who, as he crawled towards me, gazed at me with fear-filled eyes. "I didn't mean to," he stammered. "I didn't mean to. I'm not a slaver." He was crying, and as he wiped his cheeks, I noticed how much his hand shook.

"Maybe you only wounded him," I said and gently touched his shoulder as he lay down next to me.

Jack buried his head in his hands and started to sob; and I did not know what to say to him. I too had had a Union soldier in my sight and felt a desire to press the trigger. It was less than three months since we had left Bristol together. Now, that town was so far away that I had to try in order to remember it. I touched Jack again, but he only buried his head deeper in his hands. Gallant Jack, I thought silently, fearless Jack who wanted to bring a reward back to his parents. I wished for Rolf, but there was no one to help me. After a while Jack's sobs grew less loud. I moved closer to him and whispered in his ear, "I . . . I killed someone, too. I killed a northern soldier, too."

Jack turned towards me and looked long into my

eyes; and somehow I managed to meet his searching glance. I don't know whether he believed me, probably not; still, it did seem to calm him.

At two o'clock a battery of Union artillery started to batter us. At the same time, a general attack was launched against Henry House Hill. If the 33rd Virginia had not destroyed the Union battery, we would have been lost. But the 33rd were still in blue uniforms; the northern soldiers commanding the battery mistook them for their own men and did not fire upon them before it was too late. A few hours later, the Confederate Army was reinforced by fresh troops. Slowly, we stopped retreating and started to advance down the hill.

Only generals can describe battles. They can see through their telescopes and tell about the fighting by using regimental names and numbers. I saw the dirt of Henry House Hill; and I heard the noises of the firing, the screams of the wounded, and the curses of the damned. Let no man tell you of the glories of war, for what glory can there be in killing your fellowmen?

"Jim . . . Jim . . ."

I was still beside Jack, but we had not spoken to each other since he had wept for the man he had killed. In crouching positions, we were advancing with the soldiers towards the retreating northern armies.

"I am going to run . . . I am going to run, Jim." His voice trembled as if he were still crying. "If they kill me, then I won't be . . . won't be . . ." In a great rush he said, "Then I won't be a slaver anymore. If they kill me, I won't be a slaver, anymore."

I grabbed his sleeve. "But you're not a slaver anyway."

He pushed my hand away, stood up, and started to run towards the retreating northerners. The men nearest us began to follow him, and soon the entire regiment was on their feet, and screaming they rushed down the hill towards the Union lines. I ran with the rest; I was trying to catch Jack.

I did not reach him before he was hit. I saw him stumble, fall, and then roll down the hill, until his body was stopped by a small bush. He had been hit in the chest and was dead. The bullet must have gone through his heart. I spoke to him, called his name again and again, but he did not answer. Never would he climb the rigging again, to feel the wind in his face.

"A brave lad . . . I saw him." An elderly officer with a great black beard was leaning over Jack's body. There was a younger officer at his side. "Give his name to your regimental officer, so that his family can be informed . . . of . . ."

While he faltered for the right word, I looked at him and realized that it was General Jackson.

"Informed of his heroism," the young aide suggested.

The general nodded, but he looked dissatisfied, as if the words had not pleased him; then they both walked away.

I saw a flower growing nearby and plucked it. It
was a kind that also grows in England. I wanted to
place it on Jack's chest, but his chest was too bloody,
so I put it in his right hand.

I got up and followed the other soldiers down the
hill. When I had walked about a hundred yards, I
turned back. There were so many dead on the hill
that I did not know which one was Jack.

The Union forces were routed. The battle was over.
The soldiers in gray, though victorious, were ex-
hausted. The road to Centreville was open, and General Jackson wanted to pursue the defeated enemy
and take the village where they had now set up head-

quarters; but Generals Johnston and Beauregard were satisfied with the victory they had won, and the Confederate Army did not advance much beyond the stone bridge that spanned the Bull Run.

I looked everywhere for Rolf and Keith but could not find them. "If they are dead," I thought, "then I am alone." I sat down under a tree on the bank of the little river. I was looking at Henry House Hill, the troops were collecting the wounded and the dead. When I realized that I was still carrying my rifle, I put it down. I felt freer and knew that I would not pick it up again. I sat there long, until suddenly I thought almost out loud, It's getting late, Jim. Now you must go.

I rose and walked among the trees. The sun would soon be setting behind me, in the west. I had not walked a mile before the trees thinned out, and I was walking through an open pasture. A mile or so beyond it, another forest began. As I crossed the fields, fearless because I did not care what happened to me, I saw the road to Centreville; it was not half a mile away. The Union Army was moving along it. I noticed the carts and wagons that carried the wounded.

Soon I was in the woods again. I came to a creek; the water looked so clear. I took off my clothes and washed myself; then, because the water was so pleasant against my body, I sat down in the middle of the creek.

"If you washed that boy from now until New Year,

he'd be a dirty little Bristol boy, anyway."

I leapt out of the water. Rolf and Keith were standing at the edge looking at me. Though I had long since given up hope of ever seeing my comrades again, I kept repeating, as I put my clothes on over my wet body, "I knew I'd find you . . . I knew I'd find you . . ."

"We've been waiting here for hours, for you two. We got away just . . ." Suddenly Rolf stopped speaking; then he said with alarm, "Where's Jack?"

"Where's Jack?" Keith repeated.

I didn't want to tell them what had happened to Jack, for I felt if I didn't tell about him, he wouldn't be dead.

I looked up at him and now I cried.

"Sit down, boy," Keith said kindly.

I sat down on the bank of the little stream and my tear-filled eyes followed the blurred image of a leaf being carried downstream by the current; between two stones it disappeared and did not come up again.

"He's dead," I said. When I pronounced the words, I knew it was true. "I put a flower in his hand."

Keith and Rolf were silent; and though they did not press me to tell the story, slowly, haltingly, I told them what had happened. When I was finished, Rolf patted my head, but Keith the foretopman turned away for he was crying.

And Friends Must Part

19

"AND HOW DO I KNOW if there is any truth in your tale?" The lieutenant looked for a moment at the three of us and then glanced out of the window. He was young and rather handsome. His head was bandaged. This was the first time he had experienced war, and it had written with its bloody finger on his forehead.

"We have marched a long way just to tell a lie, sir," Rolf answered and looked earnestly at the officer.

"But you were in the battle . . . and on the other side." The lieutenant was not angry, but he was perplexed. "I cannot just let you walk out of here. I shall have to report your story to the captain."

Rolf had told the long story of our voyage, of the sinking of the *Four Winds,* of our march from Charleston; but only when he spoke of our presence in the southern ranks and our part in the battle did the officer show any marked interest.

Several times he interrupted Rolf. "We should have won that battle! We should have won and marched on to Richmond." Finally, he called a corporal; and we were, under armed escort, marched back to the little room, barren of furniture, where we had spent the night.

"But why won't they believe us?" Keith asked.

Rolf smiled ironically. "It is a strange story. I am not sure if I were the lieutenant I should believe it myself."

I looked out of the small window into the only street of Centreville. It was filled with soldiers; some of them were wounded. They sat along the curbing of the road as if it were a comfortable couch in a parlor, so grateful did they appear simply to be sitting down.

At noon we were given a bowl of soup and some bread. The soldier who brought the food to us stared at us so curiously that Keith remarked upon it to him.

"They say you are Confederate spies and that you are going to be hung," he explained wonderingly.

Rolf and Keith laughed at him; but when he left the room, sweat broke out on both their foreheads, and they did not look at each other, or at me.

"We are going to eat!" Rolf suddenly shouted.

"Nothing like military headquarters for rumors," Keith said and handed me one of the bowls which the soldier had left on the floor.

An hour later, a corporal came. "You are going to see the general!" he announced. Two soldiers followed him into the room.

"Aye, nothing less would do for me," Keith said. "If I am going to be flogged, let it be done by order of the admiral." He smiled good-naturedly from one to the other of the soldiers, but none smiled back. And we read on their faces that they too thought we were Confederate spies.

With a soldier on either side of us, we were

marched to a very large house. We were led into the
dining room, where we waited long to be admitted to
the parlor, which we assumed was the general's office. We watched the endless file of soldiers —
mainly, officers — who walked to and fro, each looking more important than the other. At headquarters,
even a young private, carrying a pitcher of water to a
thirsty officer, has an expression on his face that would
would suit the bearer of news of an enemy attack.
All joking, and even smiling, is banned; for this is a
temple — though yesterday it was only a well-to-do
man's home — and in such holy places only the su-
preme commanders may laugh.

We were finally brought before a colonel, not a
general. He had a red beard and his name was William
Sherman. To him, Rolf again told our story, though
he made it much shorter than he had when we were
questioned by the lieutenant, for Colonel Sherman
was not inclined to hide his impatience. He kept fold-
ing and unfolding his hands, and he only looked up
at Rolf when he spoke about the battle.

"Did any of you see Colonel Jackson, Colonel
Thomas Jackson?"

Rolf shook his head, but I blurted out, "I think he
is a general, sir."

The colonel smiled. "He deserves to be." Then he
remained silent for a long time.

"We have come to serve in your army, sir," Rolf
said desperately.

"General Jackson . . . Did you really see him?"

"He spoke to me, sir, because of Jack."

"Because of Jack?" Colonel Sherman bent forward. "What do you mean, 'because of Jack?' "

I told him about Jack; that is, I told him what Jack had done and how he had died on Henry House Hill.

When I was finished, the colonel laughed and turned to the young officer who stood behind him. "That is war, Smith: a boy running down a hill, bent on getting killed, and a regiment is routed. They did not tell you about that possibility at West Point, did they?"

"No, sir," the young officer answered.

The colonel pointed to me. "How old are you?"

I was about to say fourteen, when Rolf answered for me, "He is only twelve, sir."

"Twelve," Colonel Sherman repeated. "And why did your parents allow you to go to sea? Did you run away?"

"I am an orphan, sir." Suddenly the fact of my age seemed as unbelievable to me as it must have been to everyone else.

The colonel again turned to his young aide. "War is a machine for the production of orphans. Did they teach you that at West Point?"

The young officer smiled foolishly, but when he saw the frown on the colonel's face, he answered quickly, "No, sir," and looked away.

"The sea, sir, robs many a child of his father, in times when other men sit peacefully by their firesides," Keith said; and when the colonel did not re-

spond he added, "Aye, sir, and it is the first lesson
that is taught in the school a tar goes to."

Colonel Sherman laughed; then he looked over
his shoulder at his aide. "Officers attend a college
and only start school after they have graduated from
that college; that is why wars are so costly."

There was a knock at the door, and a major entered. In a low tone, he spoke to the colonel and then
left the room. When he had gone, Colonel Sherman
told the young officer who attended him to take us to
Lieutenant Wodsley, who would see to it that good
use was made of our wish to defend the Union.

Keith sighed so heavily that it sounded as if he had
moaned; and Rolf had to wait several seconds before
he could speak coherently. "We are grateful to you,
sir! We —"

"But the boy is too young. We cannot fight wars
with children. He will have to be sent to Washington."

We walked out of the house — free men. No matter how innocent you are, the sight of two soldiers
guarding you — one on each side — makes you feel
guilty, as if you must have committed some crime.

"You will be in Bristol soon, Jim." Keith tried to
make his voice sound as if he were envious.

"I shan't be," I replied. And then I repeated it, for
I suddenly realized how little I wanted to return to
Bristol. "I shan't be."

The next morning I was ordered to join a supply
train that was going to Washington. A corporal who

drove one of the wagons was told to look after me,
and he did, though I had no intention of trying to
escape. Our wagon was drawn by mules; we progressed
slowly, and most of the time I slept.

Keith, Rolf, and I had joked when I departed;
talked about things of no importance, as if we were

merely going on different watches. "Write to us!" Rolf had shouted. And as I jumped into the back of the wagon, I had called back, "I will!"

But now, as I lay near the tailboard of the wagon, half dozing, I suddenly realized that I did not know their full names! "Keith the Foretopman and Rolf the Cook!" I whispered aloud, and then I cried, for these were the only two people in the world that I loved, and I did not know their names. How could one be so poor and so lonely! I tried to remember if Rolf had ever mentioned his full name; he spoke so seldom of his past. All I could recall was that he came from a land far to the north of England, called Norway. "Orphans of the wind," I mumbled and then I dried my eyes; but new tears came and I hid my head in the straw.

Yet tears will stop and cheeks bathed in sorrow will dry. Those who are capable of loving will feel the pain of parting so hard that sometimes they will curse their gift; for they know not and cannot imagine the horror of the world of those who are locked in themselves, hidden in those icy caverns where a brother's laughter or his tears cannot be heard.

I fell asleep, and in my dreams I was back on the *Four Winds*. I was sitting on deck, midship, listening to Keith who was singing a Bristol song about a man who lived alone with a cat. Just as Keith had sung the last verse, Potiphar crossed the deck and sat down beside him. I laughed out loud, as did all the others; then I woke up.

"What are you laughing at, boy?" the corporal, who was sitting in the forepart of the wagon, asked.

"About a cat," I said, but knowing that my answer must have sounded silly, I added, "his name was Potiphar."

The corporal spat at the rear end of one of the mules. "You are all the way from England, aren't you?"

I got up and made my way forward to sit down beside the corporal. "From Bristol," I answered. Suddenly I was smiling, for the thought had come to me that Rolf was wrong: we were not "orphans of the wind"; we were brothers of the earth, and the wind and the sea were our parents.

Epilogue

"LET GO THE ROYALS!"

I looked up in the rigging. The sails were filling
out. The wind came from north, northwest. The sails
were white like the wings of a swan, not gray and
patched like the ones on the *Four Winds*. It was a
fine ship — a brigantine, well kept and well-trimmed
— but at the moment, I longed for the *Four Winds*.
Rolf, I thought and glanced at the men working near
me. One of them winked and smiled . . .

Tomorrow, always tomorrow. We sail into it, and
yesterday disappears like the foam in a ship's wake.
I thought of Jack. No, it was not like the foam, for
Jack sailed with me.

No one in Washington had been eager to send me
back to England. When I had said that I wanted to
sign on an American ship, the man at the embassy, to
to whom the corporal had delivered me, seemed
pleased. He sent me to Baltimore, where the English
Consul arranged for me to sail as a deck boy on the
Luck of Gloucester.

"Get those ropes on the foredeck tidy!" the second
mate called.

The tar who had winked at me joined me on the
foredeck. "Bill is the name. I'm from Maine."

"Jim," I replied and looked towards the land that was fast disappearing. Beyond the shore are Keith and Rolf, I thought; and again I felt the pain of loneliness.

"Where are you from?" Bill from Maine asked. He was coiling a rope, but his glance was upon me and he still was smiling.

"From Bristol, in England. And then, to my own surprise I added, "I was one of the crew of the *Four Winds*, a brig that was blown up down Charleston way." Bill looked at me admiringly. I judged him to be a year or two older than myself.

"Come on, children. Do you think this is a school? Stop talking and work." The second mate was standing near us.

Suddenly I grinned as I started to coil one of the ropes. We were bound for California. We would sail around Cape Horn! "And then . . . and then, you'll be a real tar, Jim," I whispered to myself.

The thought pleased me. I looked up at the mast and the little clouds high above it. The world is good, I thought. And it is mine. Mine the whole world, the sea and the wind.